UNANTICIPATED REUNION

Sweet Reunion Romance Collection, Book Three

BARBARA McMAHON

Unanticipated Reunion

1

Late July

Noelle Simpson let herself into her home slowly. It no longer felt like home, only a building where she had once had happiness. It was mid-afternoon, but the silence hung heavy as midnight.

"Trevor?" she called from habit, then stopped, remembering. Trevor would never answer again. The clutch of pain gripped her heart. Her husband of five years was dead. He'd never hold her, laugh with her, or share quiet evenings with her again.

Noelle headed for their bedroom. A shower and fresh change of clothes were in order. She'd put in another full day at the office, working to close it down. It wasn't a labor of love, but one to be mourned as she mourned her husband's passing.

The bedroom was dim, the drapes pulled against the afternoon sun. Antique furnishings and carpets were to be protected. Trevor had loved this room. She hesitated in the doorway, looking immediately at the bed almost imagining Trevor lying on top of the duvet, waiting for her.

"Trevor?" she said softly.

Of all the rooms in the house, she felt his presence most in this one.

Shrugging out of her clothes, she took a quick shower. Wrapped in a light robe, she went to crawl into bed. She wished she could pull the covers over her head and stay there forever. Taking a deep breath, she could still smell the lingering scent of him. Tears began again. She felt as if she'd cried herself out long ago, but still they came.

Rolling over, she gathered his pillow against her, burying her face in it. It wasn't fair he was gone and the pillow remained—a reminder of the man she'd loved who'd been taken too soon.

The last few months had been a blur. Coming home one day, she'd found him in bed with another killer headache. That afternoon she'd learned the truth. The headaches weren't migraines, but symptoms of a tumor that was too invasive to eradicate. Her husband was going to die within months.

She'd tried to hold on to every moment since Trevor had told her. But the immediate past was still a blur. She remembered railing against fate, urging him to consult other doctors, to find a surgeon willing to operate. To do something to stay alive.

He'd been kind, but firm. He'd already tried everything. He'd come to terms with the indictment. Noelle had not. She'd done all she could to stave off the inevitable.

When she'd finally accepted the fact, she'd stopped going to work, determined to spend every moment with him. Trevor hadn't objected.

Nor had his partner, Linc.

Closing her eyes, she could see Trevor in this bed, trying to overcome the pain, the lines etched in his face from the intensity. Only death had released the pain.

"I want you to promise me when the inevitable happens to me you'll go to Linc. He'll take care of you," Trevor had said one afternoon.

Trevor had been in his mid-fifties. He should have had decades of life ahead of him. Granted he'd been almost thirty years older than she, and she'd known in her mind that one day he'd probably die before her, but not so soon. He'd known he was dying for eight months. He'd done his best to protect her against the knowledge until there was no hiding it.

"The prognosis wasn't good from the beginning. No surgery. I could have tried radiation and chemo, but my oncologist didn't hold out any hope, so I elected not to subject myself and you to the horrors in hopes of gaining a few weeks at most. Quality counts with me, you know that," he'd told her that awful day.

"You can't die," she had repeated, shocked by his revelation.

"Noelle, you need to listen to me. This is important. I've been thinking of your future since I received the prognosis. You know most of our income is from my grandfather's trust. Even the house we live in belongs to the trust. All that ends with my death. And I don't see Paul continuing any allowance for you."

"I don't care about money!" she said hotly. He was talking about money at a time like this? "I care about you. I love you. I can't go on if you're not here."

Noelle knew his older brother Paul had never liked her. But that was the least of her concerns at this moment. She couldn't accept that Trevor was dying!

"Of course you will. You're young, healthy and have years of happiness ahead of you. You need to listen to me now. I have it figured out. I've done my best to put aside some money for you over the last few months, without alerting Paul by drawing down extraordinary amounts. But it's not enough. Linc and I began that expansion last year, unfortunately just before I received the diagnosis. So much of my personal income and assets went to that expansion and are now tied up in the company. I can't ask Linc to buy you out yet. It's a crucial junction for the firm. I know the expansion is going to pay off. You've seen the reports. I need you to promise me you'll let everything stay the way it is for a year. Just a year. That gives Linc time to establish the business we both know is there, to start reaping the benefits. He can buy you out after that if you like. Or you can stay in the firm. You get my shares. You'll be a full partner."

"Oh, Trevor," she sobbed against the pillow. "You did your best. But I need you. I miss you so much."

Her stay in the house was ending. Paul had given her two months to vacate and the deadline was only days away.

Conscious of her promise to Trevor, of all the implications, she wished she'd not given it. Trevor's partner rubbed her the wrong way. Not initially. When she'd first gone to work at Simpson and Mathias as a secretary six years ago, she'd enjoyed working with both partners.

Linc had been only a few years older than she, with tons

of terrific ideas, and a determined drive that assured his success.

Trevor was the older, more cautious partner, and the one who had handled most of the financing.

It was only after she fell in love with Trevor, and then married him, that her relationship with Linc had subtly changed.

He and Trevor's brother, Paul Simpson, had been convinced she married Trevor for his money. As if. It didn't matter a bit to her that he'd been almost thirty years her senior. She loved him and she knew he loved her.

She'd continued to work after their marriage, progressing to office manager. She knew almost as much about the firm as Trevor did. He often discussed things with her and even implemented her ideas from time to time. Maybe she should have left and found a job with a different firm. Then he wouldn't have put any restrictions on her or urged her to depend on Linc.

Shortly after their marriage, Linc had relocated to San Francisco, opening a branch of their security firm on the West Coast. The firm had recently expanded into some of the Pacific Rim countries. Trevor had continued with the operation in Washington, D.C.

Fortunately for peace in the partnership, she and Linc had rarely seen each other over the last few years. Designing and installing state of the art security measures was a growing business as the threat of terrorism grew. Their specialty was training businessmen in how to be safe in foreign settings, to minimize danger when away from home, and protect themselves in daily life.

It wasn't enough she was losing her home. Trevor had extracted another promise.

"I want your promise you'll work with Linc for a year. Put your efforts into helping him make the company the success I know it can be. Consolidate to reduce expenses. Close the D.C. office. Move to San Francisco. Work with Linc."

She'd argued against it, knowing she'd work better with Linc if there was a continent between them. In the end, she'd given in. She'd have done anything to make his last days happy. He was dying. She hadn't wanted to talk about business.

At least she'd talked Trevor out of the harebrained notion he'd voiced one time.

"One way to protect the assets of the company and to make sure you two are pulling together as a team would be to marry," Trevor had said pensively.

She stared at Trevor. "You're crazy. That tumor has affected your mind. I'm not going to marry Linc Mathias."

"He'll succeed, you know he will. And if you two were married, you wouldn't have to dissolve the partnership later or fragment the business. I don't want Paul making any trouble. I don't want you floundering when I'm gone. I want to know you'll be taken care of. Give me that one promise, Noelle. Please."

It had been the one promise she couldn't make.

She cried herself to sleep, Trevor's voice echoing around her.

Linc Mathias hung up the phone and leaned back in his chair. It was after seven on a Thursday night and he was still at the office. He got more done when the place was empty and the phones quiet. Still, if the phone rang, he'd answered it as he had a few moments ago.

Robert Wiley had called to report in on Noelle. Robert was an operative in the D.C. office. Linc had asked him to keep an eye on Noelle while she worked through closing the office and the home she and Trevor had shared.

He'd called to report the last of the details had been seen to. As of Monday, the office would be vacated, a sub-lessee already lined up.

Linc rose and strode to the window to gaze out, not seeing the outline of the Bay Bridge spanning the San Francisco Bay, nor the high rise office buildings of the financial district. Instead he saw his friend the last time they'd been together in March. Trevor had exacted Linc's promise to take care of Noelle. Sick with worry and regrets, Linc had agreed. Now the reality of that promise was coming home to roost.

Noelle.

She'd be moving to San Francisco soon. He'd see her every day. Would she fit in or constantly be a thorn in his side?

Trevor's idea sucked. If Linc hadn't known Trevor was ill, that stupid scheme would have convinced him. Take care of Noelle, give her a role in keeping the business intact? Treat her like a full partner? Not likely. He'd find a way to buy her out. He wasn't going to get tangled up with her. If Trevor wasn't going to be involved, he wanted to run the business all by himself.

Trevor had been the more cautious partner, really delving into things before agreeing to major changes. Did he really expect Noelle to assume his role? She was only twenty-eight; she didn't begin to have the business experience Trevor had brought to the firm.

When their young secretary had married the boss five years ago, Linc had been convinced she'd done so to latch onto the Simpson millions. After five years of marriage, however, Linc wasn't so sure.

Noelle worked hard at the D.C. office.

As far as he knew she'd always been faithful to Trevor and seemed to hold her much older husband in high regard. She hadn't blown money on expensive clothes or jewels or trips to Europe.

Maybe he'd misjudged her five years ago.

Still, a twenty-eight-year-old woman with a fifty-five-year-old man wasn't a likely match made in heaven.

She was probably wishing now that she could have found a way to get some of the family trust money before Trevor was gone. Paul would see to it she didn't get a cent. Trevor had complained often about how Paul disliked Noelle. Linc knew Trevor's brother had already given her notice to vacate the family home, although it had been expected. One of Trevor's regrets at the end was that he hadn't provided better for Noelle and he was depending on Linc to do so.

Linc didn't have a problem keeping an eye out for her. He just didn't want her involved with Simpson and Mathias.

Though he'd promised his friend he'd see to that exact thing. He'd promised, but could he deliver? Especially with

Trevor's idea of keeping her on as a partner until the company was doing well enough for Linc to buy out her half without jeopardizing what they'd built?

"There are ways to safeguard your wife's interests without making her a part of the firm," Linc muttered.

Linc had put all he had, and all he could borrow, into expanding the company. The early returns showed great potential. Facing facts realistically, he knew they couldn't absorb the expenses Trevor's trust normally took care of. Which meant no money to provide a place for Noelle to live. No second office in D.C. No way for her to stay with the company unless she moved to California.

He didn't want Noelle within three thousand miles of him.

And not only because of his discomfort every time he thought about her marrying his partner, but because of the pure sexual attraction he'd felt when she was around. Linc had done his best to ignore it. Avoid her whenever he could. He and Trevor were partners, not he and Noelle.

Trevor had asked the impossible.

And Linc had promised to deliver.

2

August

Noelle gazed out the airplane window. They were cruising at something like six miles up. She'd heard the announcement, but it hadn't really registered. From here, however, the heartland of America looked like some pattern in green and brown. Leaning back in her seat, she gazed at the sparse clouds dotting the horizon. In only a little longer she'd be landing in San Francisco.

She wondered whether the years had softened Linc's belief that she'd married Trevor for his money.

Nothing had softened Paul's.

He'd told her on the day after the funeral to vacate the family home immediately. When Linc, standing nearby, had heard, he'd argued on her behalf. Paul had grudgingly given her two months to move out. Only, she was sure, because of the pressure Linc had brought to bear.

She'd packed her few things and left the house immaculate.

The nest egg that Trevor had built for her was safely in the bank. She hoped she wouldn't need to use it any time soon, but it was there. A last gift from her husband.

Leaving the house had been hard, but only because of the happy memories she retained from her marriage.

The Virginia side of the Simpson family had inherited wealth from generations of men who seemingly had the Midas touch. Trevor's grandfather, in order to safeguard that wealth, had tied up the family money in a trust to be doled out to each generation. She and Trevor had had no children, so there was no more Simpson money once he died.

As if she cared. She'd loved her husband and deeply grieved his passing. No matter what Paul thought, she'd made Trevor happy for the five years of their marriage.

Yet a slow anger smoldered inside her that Trevor had extracted that promise from her to work with Linc for a year. She didn't want to be tied up with Lincoln Mathias for twelve months. Didn't want to have to endure his scorn and dislike for a single day.

She could renege—Trevor was gone, he'd never know.

But that didn't feel right. She'd made the promise in order to ease his last days. She wouldn't back out now—she'd know she'd broken her word and she couldn't live with that.

Somehow she and Linc had to make this work. She'd talk to him when she landed and hopefully come to some kind of compromise. Once she arrived in San Francisco, she'd have lots to do. She needed to find a small apartment. Arrange for her few pieces of furniture to be delivered. Find a niche for herself within the firm.

While she'd continued working for the company after she had married Trevor, it had been as an employee. Now she had her husband's shares. On paper she was an equal partner with

Linc Mathias. That would certainly change the dynamics. She almost looked forward to butting heads with the man. That would take her mind off losing Trevor.

The thought filled her with a quiet satisfaction. If Linc thought he could browbeat her into going along with all his ideas, wouldn't he be in for a surprise? The anger that flared was cathartic. It had been her job to close the Washington office and she had accomplished the task expediently and efficiently. She had learned a lot from Trevor. Linc would find she could pull her own weight.

Noelle had spoken to Linc a couple of times on the phone since the funeral. She wondered what was going on in the San Francisco office that she should know about. It'd take her a little while to come up to speed. She'd visited that office a couple of times over the years. Usually Trevor had left her in charge of the Washington office while he went west to confer with Linc. Only twice in the years they were married had Linc come to D.C.

Linc had told Noelle to take her time moving to California. But she needed something to fill her days and make her tired enough to sleep at night. The sooner she started work, the sooner the year would be up.

To Noelle's surprise, Linc was waiting in the baggage claim area in the airport when she came off the concourse. He stepped up and took her carry-on bag.

"Good flight?" he asked, turning and gesturing toward the conveyor belt of rotating baggage.

"Yes, thank you."

He was several inches over six feet and always seemed to

tower over her, though she herself was a bit above average height. His dark hair gleamed in the artificial light, worn longer than Trevor. He moved with a gracefulness that always reminded her of a panther–no wasted motion, ready to pounce.

He wasn't an easy man to be around, given more to sardonic comments, impatient and challenging statements than genial conversation. But he did keep her on her toes.

She planned to prove to him that Trevor's trust in her had been justified. She wanted Linc to one day tell her that Trevor's request had been the best thing that had happened to the company. She knew she had a lot of ground to cover before then and hoped Linc was open-minded enough to let her do what she'd come for.

If not, it was only for a year. She could stick the course for one year.

"I reserved a room at that hotel on Market Street that Trevor liked," she said as they stood with the crowd waiting for the luggage to arrive. She couldn't help remembering that the last time she'd flown to San Francisco. Trevor had been with her.

"I'll drop you," he said. "Since today is almost shot, you may wish to rest up tomorrow. If so, don't worry about coming into the office."

"I napped on the flight," she said. "I'll be there bright and early ready to work"

He moved impatiently. "Look, Noelle, I know Trevor and you worked closely in the Washington office, but I'm used to being in charge here. I don't need an in-my-face partner to dog my every move."

Noelle was taken aback but determined not to show it. What else had she expected from Linc other than hostility?

"I'm here to take on my new role in the company. Trevor and I reviewed everything before his death. I know exactly where we stand, the vision you and he had for expansion, and the pitfalls with competitors, the market and the changing world situation. I'm not some hothouse flower needing coddling, despite what Trevor thought," Noelle insisted. "I know he could be a little old-fashioned in his views, but I'm perfectly capable of handling my share of the firm. In fact, I wanted to talk to you about the new efforts in software security. There are lots of firms out there that produce a good solid product, so why are we diverting our resources into that area? I think we need to re-examine our direction and purpose, and stick to a course for a period of months to make sure we strengthen our core product—which is *personal* security."

"To stay competitive, we have to offer a full, turn-key program, suitable to *all* who want our services. This includes computer security," Linc explained. "But this is not the time or place for this discussion. If you have some legitimate concerns, we'll discuss them at the office. But if you're just trying to throw your weight around, forget it. Check the long-range plans we devised before the expansion. This was a key feature."

The carousel started and luggage began to appear. Noelle had to keep a close eye for her bags, as so many looked alike these days. She might have known Linc would argue with her first statement. He was right, however, her timing was bad. That discussion was for the office, not an airport terminal.

She appreciated his picking her up. It saved her the hassle of taking a taxicab into San Francisco. Soon he'd drop her at the hotel and she'd be on her own again. She just had to be cordial for a little longer.

And, from his earlier comments, ready to go to battle when she reached the office in the morning.

When her bags arrived, he grabbed the two she indicated.

"Is this it?" he asked.

"Yes. The rest of my things, including the furniture I was entitled to, are coming by moving van. I hope to find a place to live before they arrive or everything will have to go into storage."

"Maybe you should have left everything in Washington. You'll be going back in a year, right?"

She nodded as he led the way to the parking garage. That was the plan. In a year, she hoped the firm would be doing so well that they could reopen the D.C. office and she'd return home in a heartbeat.

In only a short time Linc reached a black sports car and opened the minuscule trunk. Depositing her two suitcases into it was a tight fit, but he managed to get them both in.

"You'll have to bring the carry-on up front with us," he said, going around to unlock the passenger door.

Seated in the comfortable, sexy car a moment later, Noelle wished she could relax and enjoy the ride. The car she and Trevor had leased had been a big sedan. Turned in, of course, after his death. It had been nothing like this.

Would her income allow her to get something fun to drive? That was another issue to discuss. Trevor hadn't taken a salary from the company, plowing his earnings back into the business. His income from the trust had enabled him to live comfortably without his salary.

Noelle, on the other hand, had only her salary as office manager which ended when the office closed. She'd need income from Simpson and Mathias—starting right away!

Linc quickly exited the airport, slipping into the flow of traffic heading for San Francisco.

"I've called a staff meeting at eleven tomorrow morning, pending your decision to come in or not. You know most of the people in the office at least by phone," he said. "That way you can meet everyone and we can establish our parameters."

"Meaning?"

"I'm not your adversary, Noelle," he said evenly. "You and I are equal partners in Simpson and Mathias. We need to establish a united front for the staff and clients. Any differences between us must be worked out behind closed doors."

"You're right. Do we have differences?"

Beside the software development aspect and the fact she hadn't wanted to close the Washington office, she thought.

He glanced at her, his dark eyes narrowed slightly. She felt a catch in her breath. Darn it, she didn't need this. Every time she was around him, she felt breathless, like she was mesmerized by his dynamic personality. She was used to being around men—after all, the operatives in the Washington office had been mostly male. None of them had ever disturbed her like Linc did.

Why hadn't Linc married, she wondered. He was in his

mid-thirties. To her knowledge he'd never even come close to marriage. Why not?

"I don't know, you tell me," he said in that low deep voice.

"No differences that I know of, except the software. I plan to continue with Trevor's directions. If you have a different agenda, then we may have a problem," she said.

She had copious notes in her briefcase. Trevor had gone over everything with her prior to his death, coaching her to be all she could as a partner. To make sure Linc found no room for complaint.

He gave a shrug and drove without speaking until they reached Market Street. She studied the tall buildings that whizzed by as he navigated through the city traffic. In only a moment, he stopped in front of the hotel. A bellman came to open her door.

Trevor had loved the location. A short walk would take her to Union Square, the Embarcadero, or to Chinatown. She got out of the car.

With her luggage taken care of a few moments later, Linc said, "I'll see you in the morning, then. Unless you want to go to dinner tonight?"

"Is that part of your promise to Trevor to take care of me?" she asked lightly.

She'd find a way to let Linc know he needn't take that promise too seriously. Smiling as politely as she was able, she shook her head.

"I'm perfectly capable of taking care of myself. Thank you for the offer, but I want an early night. Maybe some other time."

He inclined his head slightly. "As you like. See you in the morning, then. You know how to find the office?"

She nodded then watched as he got into the car and quickly melded into the traffic, and was soon lost from view. Turning she entered the hotel, wishing once more with all her heart that Trevor was with her—if only to help her deal with Linc.

She was already exhausted from being with him for the length of their trip into the city and he'd hardly said a single word. It was her own keyed-up emotions, her own rising defense against her attraction to him that came unwanted.

She was mourning her husband. How could she be the slightest bit interested in even looking at another man, especially one she knew so well?

It was jet lag. Or fatigue playing tricks on her psyche, or the reaffirmation of life despite her husband's death a couple of months ago.

Whatever, she thought, as she entered the large hotel, she was not going to allow herself to be swayed by the first good-looking man she saw. She had the rest of her life before her, she'd do what she could to make sure Trevor would have been proud of her.

But the fluttering feeling that started when Linc met her at the airport hadn't diminished. She realized she was physically aware of him on all levels.

And she hated it.

Maybe being around him full-time for days on end would end that. She certainly hoped so!

Linc pulled into the underground garage of his apartment building on Nob Hill, parking in his reserved space. He got out of the car and stalked to the elevator, still fuming. Noelle rubbed him the wrong way, no doubt about it. He'd tried to do the right thing, offering to have her rest up before starting into work, but from her reaction, someone would think he was trying for a palace coup.

Not that he wanted her involved with the business. He'd always miss Trevor and his business acumen, but the company had been Linc's baby from the get-go. He'd gotten out of Special Forces with a strong awareness of the growing problem with safety of Americans on foreign soils. He'd planned the direction of his security firm, solicited venture capital—and fallen in with Trevor Simpson. It was Linc's direction and vision leading the company. He knew how to keep the accounts in the black and the firm growing at the same time.

Trevor had been the cautionary note in the partnership. Always deliberating over decisions, looking into all aspects before agreeing. Linc used a gut instinct approach and so far it had served him well.

Miss Jumped-Up-Secretary-Turned-Co-owner would soon see she was in over her head.

He knew he'd promised Trevor to take care of her, not that he thought Noelle needed any help. That didn't mean abdicating his own plans to keep her happy. She fell in with his ideas or she could draw a salary for sitting as far from the office as he could find a place.

Which reminded him, he needed to make sure she was on

the payroll at a salary befitting a partner not the Washington office manager.

When Linc reached the nineteenth floor, he stepped out and went to his apartment. Entering, he glanced around for the first time wondering what Noelle would think if she ever saw it. The few times she'd accompanied Trevor to San Francisco, they'd stayed in a hotel—the same one she was staying in tonight. When Trevor came alone, he always bunked in with Linc, using the second bedroom.

The place was modern with clean lines and furnishings to match. Linc hadn't done much to dress up the place. It was a place to eat and sleep. He spent most of his waking hours at the office or on the road.

Or at the apartment of his girlfriend du jour, as Trevor used to tease.

He closed his eyes for a moment–he missed the man. Even his nagging to find a woman to settle down with and build a family would be missed.

Linc wondered why Trevor and Noelle hadn't started a family. Was there anything to the long-ago thought that she'd married him for his money and so didn't want to bother with children?

He didn't think so.

He flung himself down on the sofa, stretched out his legs. Trevor had been happy with Noelle. And Noelle had not played the part of gold digger. She'd stayed working in the business, moving up through the ranks through her own ability, not as a favor to the boss's wife. Trevor had said more than once over the last year how much he depended on Noelle and her judgment. Was it a prelude to the change he'd known was coming?

Or had he meant it? How much of the recent decisions had been Trevor's and how many Noelle's?

Could her business sense be counted on?

Only time would tell.

Noelle took a quick shower which helped rejuvenate her. She unpacked one bag, hoping she'd be able to find a place of her own before long. She'd asked one of the secretaries in the office to find her some possible apartments that she could look at during the coming week. Betty had faxed the listings to her last Friday and she'd studied the information on the flight out. Maybe she'd take an afternoon or two off this week to look at a couple that had caught her eye.

There was so much to do. She didn't want to slack off from work and give Linc any reason to think she wasn't able to handle the job. But she did need to get settled.

When the phone rang, she hesitated answering. Who'd be calling her? Linc, of course. He was the only one who knew she was here. Not sure she was up to sparring with him again, she reluctantly lifted the receiver.

"Hello?"

"Noelle, this is Paul Simpson. I had the worst time tracking you down. I finally called Linc yesterday and he told me you'd be at this hotel today. There are some discrepancies in the books I've had audited. You and I need to have a talk about some of the expenditures Trevor made over the last year."

Trevor had warned her Paul would do all he could to make her life miserable with him not there. Was this just an opening salvo? What else would he come up with?

"I rarely had anything to do with Trevor's finances. I had my own salary from the company. He took care of our household expenses."

Trevor had coached her on what to say if Paul questioned anything. In his opinion, Paul felt every dime of the Simpson Trust deserved to stay in the accounts. Trevor's philosophy was to use what he could to enjoy life; it had also been his grandfather's premise. The old man hadn't wanted to limit his descendants, just make sure the money didn't end up being wasted.

She wasn't sure where the trust stood, but it had nothing to do with her. Trevor had kept most of that from her.

Of course she knew he'd taken more out the last year than he'd actually needed in order to build a small nest egg for her. But she didn't plan to tell Paul that. It had been Trevor's decision and she'd abide by it.

"There are a lot of things not normally part of his spending pattern. Like a diamond necklace he bought you for your birthday just days before he died. Don't you think that was a little extravagant? Especially given the circumstances?" Paul continued.

She remembered Trevor's delight with the gift, only a few weeks after he'd told her about his illness. He had said he wished he could give her a new necklace every birthday for the rest of her life. But he couldn't, so this was to last her forever.

"He chose that gift, I didn't ask for it," she said, gripping the receiver. "Paul, Trevor never once abused his privileges with the trust. He didn't try to break the terms or rail against the restrictions. If his lifestyle didn't meet your approval, that's too bad. But he was entitled to do as he wished with his portion. The time to question things was when he was alive, not now."

She hung up the phone, feeling shaky.

It rang again a moment later. She snatched it up, still annoyed Paul was harassing her. "I don't want to talk about it any more. If you have a problem, formalize it and send it to my attorneys." Not that she had any attorneys, but she guessed she could use the ones the company used.

"Whoa, pretty big guns for any situation, much less an invitation to dinner," Linc said.

"Linc?"

"Who did you think was calling?"

"I thought it was Paul again."

"He was looking for you yesterday," Linc said.

"He reached me just a few minutes ago. And had the gall to challenge me on how Trevor spent his money."

"Ever the philanthropist, our Paul. Trevor always had plenty to say about his tight-fisted brother. What did Paul say that has you so riled up? No, wait, don't tell me yet. I called to see if you'd changed your mind about dinner. I know you said no before, but I was thinking just burgers and fries or something like that. Nothing fancy. It's your first night in San Francisco, please come to dinner with me."

Noelle knew he was trying to fulfill Trevor's request to take care of Noelle, but after Paul's call, she could use something to divert her. Who better than Linc?

"All right. But I really do want to make an early night," she said, anxious to leave the hotel room and its confining space. "Shall I meet you someplace?"

"Want to eat at a restaurant on the Wharf?"

"Yes."

She loved the seafood selection available on Fisherman's Wharf.

"It won't be too crowded on a Sunday evening. I'll swing by in about forty minutes. You can then tell me all about Paul, and we'll figure out what to do about him," Linc said.

"I'll be waiting out front."

Paul was on the trail, as Trevor had predicted. And her unlikely ally was Linc. Amazing.

"Trevor, I wish you were here," she whispered as she went to brush her hair. Would she ever stop missing him with an ache so deep it seemed to go to her very soul?

The late August afternoon was breezy with wisps of high, cool fog drifting in from the ocean. Quite a change from the heat and muggy humidity of Washington. Standing on the sidewalk outside the hotel a short time later, Noelle was glad she'd been in San Francisco in summer before. She knew to bring a jacket. The days were incredibly beautiful, but the evenings could turn chilly in a hurry when the fog rolled in from the Pacific.

When Linc's car swooped to the curb, the doorman opened the door for her and she slid in. Linc still wore the pants and sports jacket he'd had on earlier. She settled in, hoping her casual attire would fit in wherever they went.

"There's a small place on the wharf that caters more to locals than the tourists. Their clam chowder is great and they always have catch of the day," he said as he headed for Fisherman's Wharf.

"Sounds good. I want some sourdough bread, too," she said, remembering how much she loved San Francisco's famous bread.

"A must, of course," he said.

She slowly let out her breath. Maybe the evening would be okay. He didn't seem as antagonistic as he had been at the airport. She'd try to imagine they were just two casual friends going to eat together, not reluctant partners who had issues they may not be able to fully resolve.

"I'm interested in what Paul had to say, but let's save that until after we order," Linc suggested.

"Fine with me. How long have you had this car?"

"A couple of years. Not much good if I want to carry more than one person, but I love it on the hills. When I take a drive along the coast, I put down the top and feel the wind whipping by," Linc said with enthusiasm.

"I'd love that," she said, picturing him speeding along the coast highway, the ocean on one side, the wind in his hair. She knew he'd handle the speed with confidence and competency, like he handled everything else.

"I'll take you with me one day," he murmured.

"Oh, I wasn't fishing for an invitation," she said, wondering if she'd have to watch her words every minute around him.

"I know. It's fun, though. You might like it."

What if I start to like you? she wondered silently. For some reason she wanted to keep their relationship purely business.

She was again experiencing that fluttering. She felt nervous, unsure of herself. For heaven's sake, she was a grown woman, too old and sophisticated to feel giddy being around a sexy man.

And Linc was definitely sexy. His eyes had that bedroom look that made her think of rumpled sheets and slow jazz. He moved with a grace not often seen in men, silent and sleek. It came from his Special Forces training, she knew. Still, it had a curious effect on her equilibrium. He seemed like the perfect loner, a man any woman would find a challenge to entice.

Not that Noelle thought about that. At least not since her first few days at Simpson and Mathias, when Linc still worked in the Washington office and she'd had a brief crush on the younger partner.

She gazed at the facades of the piers along the Embarcadero, trying to not to think about Linc and how he'd always affected her. Even happily married to Trevor, there was always something that disturbed her senses when Lincoln Mathias was around.

She had to get hold of her imagination. He was just a guy, her partner for at least the next year. There would be nothing else between them. How could there be? She still loved Trevor.

"How are you holding up?" Lincoln asked. "I should have helped close the D.C. office, but the Sand's situation almost blew up in our faces and I needed to be here."

"I'm fine. I guess I'll always miss Trevor."

"He died too young," Linc said. He reached the multilevel parking structure near the Wharf and slipped into the short line.

Noelle nodded.

"You two never had kids. Didn't you want any?" he asked casually as they inched along.

"We talked about it last winter. I did want children, but Trevor said he wasn't ready. He'd already been given the diagnosis then, of course, though I didn't learn that until much later. I wish I'd pushed harder. Maybe he would have told me sooner."

"Or me. I never suspected," he said. "He was my best friend and I never even suspected."

Noelle looked at him, surprised by the anguish in his voice. She knew Trevor had loved Lincoln like a brother—more, actually, than he'd liked Paul. But she hadn't realized it had gone so strongly both ways.

Impulsively she reached out and touched his arm. "We'll both miss him for a long time, I think," she said softly.

He shrugged off her touch.

Noelle pulled back her hand and gazed out the window. So much for trying to establish a rapport with the man.

The restaurant was small and comfortably full, not crowded. They didn't have to wait for a table.

Once they'd ordered, Linc looked at her.

"So tell me about Paul," he invited.

"He called to say he'd had the trust accounts audited. His brother has only been dead two months and he's already auditing accounts? The man's warped."

"I've always thought so. He resents you."

"I know. Trevor knew it, too."

She toyed with her water glass, wondering if she dare trust Linc. But if she wanted to gain his trust in her, she needed to offer her own.

"Paul may have some cause," she continued slowly, looking at him, trying to judge how he would take her revelation.

"About?"

"You know the terms of the trust? The income goes to the heirs. Once they die, the income stops. There is nothing there for widows or widowers of the direct heirs. There is for any children the couple may have had as they would carry on the Simpson line."

"So if you'd had children, they would have continued to receive money?" Linc asked.

"Right. Trevor knew the minute he died the money stopped and I'd get nothing. The trust owned our home even. So once he got the news from the doctor, he began drawing down a bit more each month to put in savings for me. It's not a lot, but it does give me a small cushion against an emergency. I can earn what I need, but it's nice to have that little bit just in case."

"I'm surprised Trevor didn't do more," Linc said slowly.

"What money he had, apart from the trust, he invested in Simpson and Mathias," she said. "What I'm worried about is if Paul can sue me for the extra money Trevor took from the trust for me. Trevor was entitled to it, as I understand how the trust worked. But I don't know all the terms of the trust. Since he didn't actually use the money himself, but put it into a savings account in my name, could that be in violation of the rules? What do you think?"

"Paul may try, but unless Trevor changed substantially, he wouldn't have put you in that position. He was the cautious one in the partnership, remember? He had to know whatever he was doing was within the terms and limits of the trust."

She nodded, relieved. Linc was right—Trevor had always made sure things went the way they should, never taking extraordinary risks or venturing into shady areas. If he thought it was legitimate, it would have been.

"I hoped I'd seen the last of Paul the other day when he came to the house for the key. I'm sure he changed the locks that very afternoon," she said wryly.

Linc frowned. "The man has no tact."

"He couldn't wait for me to be gone."

"What happens to the house now?"

"Good question. Paul and Elaine have their own place so they didn't want to live in Trevor's house themselves. It'll probably just sit there empty until one of their sons is old enough to have a house of his own."

"Paul's a fool. He should have let you stay there in exchange for keeping it up. But it's not our problem. If he calls you again, tell him to talk to me," Linc said.

"I can handle my own life," Noelle said sharply. She hadn't told Linc the situation for him to take over.

He looked at her, amusement dancing in his dark eyes. "Then if you ever feel you can't handle Paul, send him my way. I'd love to settle things with him on Trevor's behalf."

Noelle wondered what he'd say or do to put Paul in his place. She'd love to be a fly on the wall for that conversation.

"I have a shortlist of available apartments," Noelle said, changing the subject.

She took the paper from her bag and handed it to Linc. "Tell me which ones you think I should investigate. I don't know neighborhoods in the city yet and don't want to bother visiting any that wouldn't be a good choice."

He began to look through the list. The waiter delivered their clam chowder as he was scanning the addresses.

Noelle took a small spoonful. It was hot, but delicious. Stirring it slowly, she waited impatiently for it to cool.

He tossed her the list.

"The only one I'd say was suitable is the one in North Point. It's close enough to work so that you could walk on fine days and it's on public transportation for rainy days."

She looked at the list again.

"It's the most expensive one here," she said.

"Because it's in a nice area and close to downtown. The others aren't in the best neighborhoods, especially after dark. If you plan to work as needed, you'll be going home after dark sometimes. Especially in winter."

Linc began to eat his chowder, wondering how much Noelle could afford to spend on an apartment. He'd already made the decision to increase her salary as befitted a partner in the firm, which Noelle would need now that she no longer had access to the funds from the trust.

In fact, he was surprised she hadn't already brought up the subject. Maybe he'd just wait until she did.

He watched her take dainty spoonfuls of soup. Her hair flowed around her face, brushing her shoulders. The light brown had surprising highlights of gold which shimmered in the light. The sadness around her eyes was a legacy of Trevor's illness and death.

Linc remembered that the times he'd seen her over the years, she usually had a wary expression around him.

Ironic, really, when at first he'd wanted to ask her out himself. He still remembered the shock of discovering Trevor had beat him to it.

In those days he'd been arrogant enough to suspect any one preferring another man to him. Especially one so much older. He'd sided with Paul initially, thinking that Noelle had married his partner for his money.

Or had some of it been sour grapes because she'd preferred Trevor to him?

He looked at his soup lest he give into the urge to reach out and touch that soft hair. He wanted to see her happy again. He'd like her to smile at him in genuine delight once, not with those polite little smiles she now gave.

Would they ever be comfortable around each other?

He doubted it. The sexual pull he felt for Noelle hadn't diminished over the years, or with the knowledge that she was his friend's wife. He'd never done or said anything to anyone. He hoped that Trevor had never guessed. He knew Noelle hadn't. He wasn't sure she even liked him.

How ironic that now that she was free, he felt honor

bound to adhere to his friend's last wish to let Noelle work in the firm for a year, then buy her out so she could go on with her life. Back to Washington. Putting the distance of a continent between them.

"Isn't your chowder any good?" Noelle asked.

"It's fine. How's yours?"

"Delicious. I sure hope I look more like I'm enjoying it than you do," she said, her eyes twinkling. "Tell me where you live and how you found your apartment. Are there any vacancies in your building, Linc?"

"None that I know of."

For a moment he wondered what it would be like to have Noelle living in the same building. They could drive to and from work together as a matter of expediency. Maybe even shop together to save money and save her having to purchase a car.

No, that was a major dumb idea. What on earth was he thinking?

Linc kept the conversation impersonal and friendly for the remainder of the meal. He took her back to the hotel as soon as they finished. He even offered to pick her up the next morning, but she said she'd get to the office by eight on her own.

Driving home, Linc was dissatisfied with the way the evening had gone. But he didn't have a clear picture of how he'd rather it have gone.

Noelle wasn't some woman he could develop a relationship with. She was his best friend's widow and he had to remember that.

3

The next morning Linc arrived at the office early. He went into the space recently vacated by Bill Jefferson to make way for Noelle. Standing in the doorway, he wondered what she'd think of it. The furniture was essentially the same as all the other furnishings in their offices—middle grade, wooden pieces, designed more for functionality than looks. They weren't out to impress prospective clients with high end expenses, but offer a feeling of moderation and security.

The window overlooked the street. They were high enough that the traffic noise wasn't noticeable.

He wondered again how much Noelle would really contribute to the company. Was it to be a token job or would she have input that would keep the company growing?

Why should he worry? It was only for a year. By next August, he should have enough funds freed up to buy her out.

"Hi." Noelle came up behind him. "Betty said to come on back."

She sidestepped around him and entered the office. "This is mine?"

"Yes."

She walked in and put her purse on the desk, dumping a bulging soft-sided briefcase beside it. "I brought files I wanted to review with you right away," she said.

She moved behind the desk and sat in the chair, looking up at Lincoln.

"I know I'm not Trevor," she continued. "But he and I worked closely together. I'm not going to do anything to ruin this company. I'm a partner now. We need to work together," she said. In her navy blue suit with a center button on the jacket, she looked cool and professional.

Her speech sounded rehearsed. For a moment Linc relaxed. Maybe she was more nervous about their working relationship than he expected. And she wasn't trying to throw her weight around. He hoped things stayed that way.

"Just like Trevor and I worked together," Linc agreed. He'd give her a chance. If it didn't work out, he'd see what he could do to buy her out earlier.

"And that was how, exactly?"

"I decided the direction of the firm, Trevor looked for the pitfalls, reminded me to rein in my spending and generally acted as a watchdog."

She nodded. "Trevor said the company had been your idea from the word go. You have Special Forces training, an intelligence background. Frankly I don't have any idea how to keep people safe in some of the situations in the world today. I'm happy to work behind the scenes. But I still want to talk about the software idea."

"Done. Come to my office in an hour. We'll go over that and some other things. Staff meeting at eleven," he reminded her.

Linc strode off to his own office. It was the one used for client meetings; consequently it was twice as large as any other, with a round conference table by the corner windows, and a small sofa along one wall. Award plaques and discreet photos lined the back wall. He wanted people to know his firm could manage their security, yet not broadcast it to the world.

His desk was piled high with reports. When clients came, he and his secretary, Betty, cleared the desk to give it an uncluttered look. None were expected anytime soon, so the desk was in its normal chaotic state.

He sat and picked up the first report, trying to focus on the words and ignore the fact that Noelle Simpson was two doors down from him.

At nine, Betty poked her head in Linc's office. "Noelle is reviewing the reports from the field now, and asked if she can meet with you later. She wants to be up to speed when meeting with the rest of the staff at eleven."

He nodded, checking off another detail Bill Jefferson had nailed for the security of a prominent banker and his family. When Betty closed the door, he leaned back, tossing his pen on the desk. He didn't want to admit how much he'd been looking forward to hearing Noelle argue against the software development project.

He liked looking at her, liked the way she got fired up over things. Her eyes would sparkle and she'd be passionate about her side of the argument.

He rose and walked to the window. It was another beautiful day in San Francisco; clear blue skies, a slight breeze to keep the air clean. Feeling restless, he wanted to be outside. Glancing at the stack on his desk, however, he knew he had more work to do before taking off.

And there was the staff meeting at eleven. He wanted to make sure everyone was onboard with their new plan. He and Noelle had to work together, but he was still the man in charge. He didn't want any questions about that from the staff. He was gone a lot with field work, and if they thought Noelle was in charge in his absence, he needed to straighten that out at the get-go.

The meeting went off without a flaw until the end. Noelle was quiet most of the time, only asking questions to clarify a report. The rest of the staff—from the security experts to the clerical workers—all had spoken with her from time to time on various projects. While she knew them by name, he could almost feel her memorize faces to go with the voices she recognized.

Her deference to him when someone asked a question raised a red flag. She was not normally so self-effacing. Was she biding her time or was she acting as a typical newcomer? Linc almost wished she'd challenge him on something just to see her in action.

Before the meeting ended, he brought up the topic guaranteed to provoke a response.

"Hal, where do we stand on the startup of the software system?"

Noelle's gaze swiveled to his as she frowned at the question. Linc almost smiled in satisfaction at her predicted response.

"I've been interviewing some programmers," Hal said, looking from one partner to the other.

The others in the room immediately picked up on the sudden tension.

"And have you and others looked at existing software?" Noelle asked.

Hal nodded. "We'd like ours to be similar to one of the existing ones out there—but with lots more bells and whistles. And another level of encryption to keep it safe from hackers."

"So we have a pattern we like. Can't we work with that developer to get what we want on a special order?" Noelle asked.

"Too many people would be involved. It would compromise the security levels," Linc said. He'd looked into this—did she think he hadn't?

"Not if you limit the programmers involved and had them working here, but under contract with the other firm. Why reinvent the wheel?" she countered. "I don't think we need to develop our own."

He felt his irritation rise. They'd agreed to present a united front and she wasn't holding up her end of the bargain.

"It's something to consider. We'll discuss this before making any firm decisions."

Linc looked around the table. "Anything else?"

Men and women shook their heads, darting uncertain glances at Noelle.

"Thank you for coming," he said, standing. He gathered his notes and left the conference room. "Noelle, could I see you a moment?" he asked in passing.

"I'm on my way out to lunch. Maybe later," she said, avoiding his eyes.

From the silence in the conference room, Noelle knew she'd just done something astonishing. Did no one tell the boss no?

She gathered the reports, her notes and pencil and rose. Linc was still standing in the doorway looking at her. Judging by his expression, he wasn't a happy camper. And she knew why. But she wasn't going to be intimidated by him. If he thought she was just some token staff member to placate until the year was up, it was time he learned differently.

She walked to the doorway, conscious of every eye in the room on her. Smiling politely, she stopped just short of where Linc blocked the entrance. She wouldn't make a scene by pushing past him. But if he didn't move, they were stuck.

"This won't take long," he said.

"Then come have lunch with me. I'll treat. I have an appointment at two to see that apartment on North Point."

She watched him clench his jaw and then nod once before he walked out. A moment later he entered his office. She waited for him to slam the door, but he didn't even close it.

Noelle went back to her own office feeling buffeted and shaky. The meeting had gone fine. It was his last challenge that raised her ire. She didn't think they should develop their own software—there were a myriad of reasons why ordering special features to a tested product made sense.

Trevor had been as concerned.

Her office gave her no respite. It was stark and plain. If she was to work comfortably here, she wanted plants, some colorful paintings on the wall and maybe an area rug to soften the austerity. Until then, it didn't feel like hers.

She was borrowing the office for a year. Would she feel at home any time in the next twelve months? Could she and Linc work together? So far she felt as if they were walking a fine line, any jarring motion and one or the other would topple.

She didn't plan for it to be her.

She put her notes down, picked up her purse and turned to leave. She wasn't sure where to eat, but surely they could find some place on the way to North Point.

Linc joined her at the elevator. "Thought your invitation was for lunch," he said.

"Oh, you didn't really respond, so I thought the answer was no," she said sweetly, smiling to confuse the man.

"And I thought we were going to present a united front to the staff. Your ideas with the software weren't bad, but have already been considered," he said.

Going by his narrowed eyes, she knew he wasn't buying her happy front.

"You might have waited to bring up the matter until after we had discussed it. I told you when I first got here that I have reservations about creating our own software," she replied.

"You might have kept our nine o'clock appointment so I could bring you up to speed on the subject," he returned.

"Is that what you planned at that meeting?" she asked as the elevator doors opened. There were several other people already inside. "To browbeat me into compliance?"

Several faces turned their way.

Linc glanced around, frowned and faced the front.

"I would have gone over the background of the project, so you didn't need to bring up things we've already hashed out."

"I thought I should come up to speed with the reports from the operatives directly, to save you repeating everything," she said. "I didn't know the software project was imminent."

Linc had planned to tell her exactly why he wanted the new software, the ideas that had been bandied around, and why his way was best. Instead, she acted like Trevor would have.

But if she thought she'd be an actual part of the business, she had another think coming. While Noelle might have done a good job running the Washington office, that didn't necessarily make her partner material. What had Trevor been thinking?

She barely reached his shoulder. Her hair was worn free, brushing her shoulders. The honey-brown tones with their streaks of gold caught his eye. The navy suit she wore should have made her look standoffish, but it had the opposite effect on him. He wanted to remove the jacket and see what she wore beneath it. A shell? A camisole? Or only some flirty little lacy bra?

Linc watched the numbers change as the elevator descended. He could smell the light fragrance she wore. It reminded him of other days—when she'd first come to work for them in Washington. He'd wanted to ask her out, but struggled with the idea of dating an employee.

Obviously Trevor had had no such compunction. Linc still remembered how he felt when Trevor had come in one day and said he and Noelle were dating. Unconsciously Linc's hands fisted. He'd kicked himself for delaying. For once in their relationship, Trevor hadn't been the cautious one.

When the elevator stopped at the lobby, Noelle walked

out and turned toward the double doors leading to the street.

"Where's a good place to eat quickly? The meeting ran longer than I expected. I have to be at the apartment at two."

"I'll take you there. I have my car."

"I can get a cab," she said, stopping to look at him.

Linc never realized before how blue her eyes were. Deep and clear, they looked up into his with uncertainty.

"I'll take you," he reiterated.

"Why would you bother?" she asked.

"To make sure you get a good deal," he said. "You can bargain with the landlord, you know. Don't sign at the first price."

She shrugged. "No, I didn't know. I lived with roommates before I married Trevor and then we lived in his home. Thank you for the tip."

It was the least he could do for his friend. Make sure his wife—widow—didn't get rooked by some landlord asking more than he should for an apartment.

By late afternoon Noelle was frustrated beyond measure. The apartment on North Point had been small, dark and damp. She hadn't liked it at all. Lincoln had firmly vetoed the idea after seeing only the entrance and front door.

"No security," he'd said.

"I'll be fine," she'd argued, just to keep her hand in.

"We need to practice what we preach," he said smoothly, standing in the living room as she viewed the bedroom and bath.

"It's not for me," she said. "But not because of the lack of security."

The landlord had blustered that they lived in a safe neighborhood, but Linc had quoted statistics on the crime rate that had shut the man up.

He'd taken her to two other addresses on her list, more to show her what she was looking at for the price than because he thought she should seriously consider either neighborhood.

"So where should I live?" she asked when they were back in his car after the third apartment had fallen short of her expectations.

"My neighborhood, but there's nothing available I know about. I'll put out some feelers."

"Great. And in the meantime I stay in the hotel? I can't afford that indefinitely." Noelle wondered if Linc's plan was to get her so discouraged she retreated to Washington, leaving him in complete control.

He looked at her, not starting the car.

"I'm going to Vancouver later in the week and I'll be gone several days. You can stay in the guest room at my place while you keep looking. I'll have Betty try to get some other listings," he offered.

"Stay at your place?" For a moment her heart seemed to skip a beat. *Stay with Lincoln?*

"Trevor did whenever he came without you," Linc said easily.

"I know, but it's hardly the same thing."

"Relax, Noelle. I won't even be there. Take the time to

find a good place, and save some money by staying free at my apartment."

It made sense. If he were gone, why not?

"Okay, thanks for the offer. When do you leave?"

"Wednesday afternoon, after work."

"What will you be doing in Vancouver?" she asked.

"We have a prospective deal lined up with a firm up there that does a lot of work with the Asian markets. A number of Chinese from Hong Kong resettled in Vancouver. Some of the businessmen there are interested in security for travel back and forth to various cities in Asia."

"How long will you be gone?"

"A week or longer. I'm not sure."

That gave her a week to find an apartment and move. If not, she could always go back to the hotel. But at least she'd save a few dollars in the meantime. Not that money was tight yet. But she hated to dip into her savings.

Though, now that the time was at hand, she wanted to talk to Linc about her salary.

By Wednesday when Lincoln was scheduled to leave, Noelle felt more at home at the office. She was still reviewing reports from various operators. Her exposure to the operatives in Washington had been limited. This was the real heart of the organization. Had Trevor known that?

Keeping in touch with their east coast operatives also took hours each day. She went back to the hotel tired each night, but satisfied she was doing what she could for Simpson and Mathias.

Wednesday, she'd checked out of the hotel at lunch and taken a cab to Lincoln's apartment. The driver carried up her bags and placed them just inside the door.

Lincoln drove her to the apartment building after work. He'd pick up his own suitcase before heading to the airport.

"I can leave you the car," he said as they drove through the rush-hour traffic.

"I don't need it. I can get to work with no trouble and I'll take cabs when going to see prospective apartments. I'm not some green country girl unused to the big city. I'm from Washington, remember." Looking at the traffic, she knew she'd rather have someone else drive—not risk a ding on his expensive sports car.

"Okay. Just don't sign any lease until I see the place," he said.

Noelle wanted to argue, but she knew better. Lincoln had a stubborn streak a mile wide. If it made him feel better to vet her new place before she signed on the dotted line, so be it. But she'd choose the apartment and negotiate the deal. She wasn't going to depend on him.

He opened the door to the apartment. Lincoln had given her a key earlier, but she still felt very much a visitor.

"Brief tour," he said. Pointing to the left, "Kitchen and eating area. Straight ahead is the living room. Feel free to use the CD player, TV, whatever. To our right are the bedrooms." He lifted her suitcases and walked down the hall, passing two rooms and entering the last one. He put the cases near the bed, glancing around.

Noelle followed him. The large bed was centered against

the side wall. Drapes flanked the high window. There was a dresser and nightstand. Carpet on the floor muffled her steps.

"It's nice," she said politely, wondering if he had something against pictures. There were none on any walls that she could see.

"Bath through there. It also opens into the hall."

"Thank you."

He nodded and went to one of the doors he'd passed earlier. A moment later he came out carrying his own suitcase. Noelle walked into the living room, feeling out of place in the modern design. She and Trevor had used his family's furnishing, most of them antiques.

"Have a good trip," she said as he opened the front door.

Nodding his thanks, he left the apartment. She closed the door and turned; now she could explore to her heart's content, without his critical eye on her.

Surveying the living room she was struck again by the sleek masculine lines everywhere. The dark furniture was rather heavy for her tastes, but was perfect for a man like Lincoln. She was surprised there weren't pictures anywhere on the walls. No clutter marred the polished surfaces of the tables either. It looked like a photo shoot in *Modern Living* or something. Didn't the man *live* here?

She walked down the hall. The first bedroom was his. She paused in the doorway, peering in. The king-size bed dominated the room. There was a highboy dresser and a night table with a lamp. Nothing else. She stepped inside and realized immediately that she could smell him in the air. Her eyes went to his closet door, and she wondered what was inside. There was a door on the adjacent wall leading to a private bath.

Sighing softly, she turned back to the hall and went to her bedroom. Smaller than his, with a queen-size bed, it looked as stark as her hotel room. No, more so. The hotel room had had pictures of San Francisco on the walls.

She placed her suitcase on the mattress and opened the door to a large walk-in closet. Her clothes wouldn't take up a tenth of the space.

Quickly she put away her things, then went to the kitchen to make herself some dinner.

Noelle felt Linc's presence around her as she worked. The refrigerator had been freshly stocked. There were plenty of canned goods and packaged food in the pantry, but she suspected the man ate out a lot or ordered dinner delivered.

After eating, she took a quick shower and changed into casual clothes. She had the entire evening ahead of her. She went over the new listings Betty had printed out but nothing struck her fancy. Maybe she should spend Saturday wandering around the city to get a feel for the different neighborhoods.

She watched TV until almost eleven, growing bored with the last show and switching it off before it ended.

When the phone rang, she hesitated. Should she answer it? Surely Linc had an answering machine.

He did, and she could hear it from the living room.

"Noelle? Are you still up?" It was Linc.

She picked up the portable phone on the coffee table. "I am," she said.

"I forgot to tell you about the security code," he said.

"For?"

"The lock on the front door. Didn't you notice it?"

She looked at the door. Beside it was a panel of buttons.

"I do now," she said.

She and Trevor had had a similar one in their home. These men believed in security in their own homes as well as the ones they sold to clients.

"Do you need to write the code down?"

"Yes, I had better. I know, don't leave it lying around," she said before he could.

Trevor had drilled that into her often enough.

"I expected you'd know the routine," he said.

"Are you in Vancouver already?"

"Got in about twenty minutes ago. Still waiting for luggage."

"Okay, ready," she said. She jotted down the numbers on the pad. "Hold on while I give it a shot."

She carried the phone with her to the door, punching in the code. The green light was replaced by red.

"I'm armed. Just let some burglar try to come in," she said. "How was your flight?"

"Uneventful. What did you do this evening?"

"Fixed dinner. You have a lot of food. Bought for me?"

"I eat, too," he said, evading a direct answer.

"Then I watched some TV. I got bored, however, and was about to go to bed."

"I won't keep you. Call me if you need anything."

The call had cheered her somewhat. She was feeling lonely. At home she had friends and activities and, of course, for the last five years, she'd had a husband.

Slowly she turned off the lights and went to the bedroom. She hadn't worked through all the stages of grief yet, but with the change of scenery, change of work and standing up to Linc all the time, she wasn't as sad and lonely as she had been those first weeks after Trevor's death.

What was Linc doing tonight? Having a quick drink at a bar before going to bed? Or reviewing the proposal he was giving to the consortium in the morning? She knew so little about him when she thought about it.

Would he think about her at all tonight?

Noelle felt the subtle difference in the office Thursday and Friday with Lincoln gone. The atmosphere was more relaxed. Everyone worked, but that edge she'd come to expect was missing. Employees took things just a little easier without Linc around.

She found some nice prints at a shop nearby on her lunch break one day, and they now hung on her wall, providing colorful contrasts to the austerity of the furnishing. Two potted violets sat where they got the most light and one was in full bloom. The rich purple color was one of her favorites.

Her role was still not clear. She had read every recent report in an attempt to come up to speed on the clients serviced from this office. She kept in constant contact with the employees now working from their homes in the D.C. area. But her days didn't feel as full as she had hoped. Hadn't Trevor had more involvement? He'd seemed to spend hours on the phone, talking with operatives, with clients. Maybe she should take on a larger role with the clients.

Friday night she ordered a pizza and ate it while watching

an old movie. She needed to make some new friends. It was hard to keep in touch with those in Washington. Because of the time difference, by the time she got home, they were getting ready for bed. Once settled in her new apartment, she'd meet her neighbors, scope out neighborhood activities. Maybe get a dog or cat.

No, not a cat. Too stereotypical of an old maid. Which she wasn't.

For a moment panic flared. Would she remain single the rest of her life? She was still young, some of her friends back at home hadn't even married for the first time, and she didn't consider them old maids, just busy career women who hadn't met their true love yet. She had met hers early—and lost him far too soon.

Or had Trevor really been her one true love? That concept gave her pause. She'd loved him. She missed him, but there was something in her that yearned for a nebulous feeling she'd never known. She couldn't imagine marrying anyone else, yet also couldn't envision living by herself the rest of her life.

Feeling melancholy, she switched off the TV and hunted through Linc's CD collection for some music to feel sad to. Finding some Coltrane, she put it on and let the mournful sounds of his sax seep in. She wouldn't have thought Linc to be a jazz fan. She flipped through his collection. He had eclectic tastes. Some were CDs she'd had at home. Others she wanted to try. Who would have thought Linc was the kind of man to sit still long enough to listen to music? He always seemed to be full of energy, kept tightly leashed in most instances. Was that part of his allure?

Not allure, she scoffed, turning away from the collection and going to lie on the sofa. He was a dynamic man. Great in the looks department. And he knew how to make someone feel special. Women would naturally be drawn to such a person. It meant nothing that she sometimes felt that special tug.

But when she tried to remember Trevor, it was Linc's face that appeared in her mind's eye.

Sometime in the night Noelle woke. She heard a noise in the front part of the apartment. Hadn't she set the alarm? She was sure she had. Rising quietly, she went to the door and listened. She heard another sound. Someone was in the apartment!

She leaned against her door, trying to see in the darkened bedroom. She'd left the apartment phone in the living room and her cell was in her handbag, also in the living room.

Was there anything she could use as a weapon if she needed to defend herself? Her heart raced. If she kept quiet, maybe the intruder wouldn't come back to the bedroom.

How likely was that? If it was a robber, he'd check out all the rooms, to get as much loot as he could.

The blood pounding in her ears made listening difficult. Was he coming down the hallway?

She took a deep breath and tried to calm herself enough to think. Slowly she rotated, opening the door a crack to hear better. She was afraid it would squeak or something, but it moved silently.

The light was on in the kitchen. Noelle heard water running. Frowning, she eased out into the hallway. Maybe she could get to a phone before whoever was here came from the kitchen.

She heard metal on metal. What was going on?

She kept close to the wall creeping down the hall to the living room. Pausing just before she dashed for her purse, she saw the suitcase in the light coming from the kitchen.

"Linc?" she ventured.

He came to the kitchen door.

"Did I wake you?" he asked.

She sank on the arm of the chair, her hand over her still-racing heart. "You about scared me to death. I thought there was a burglar," she gasped. "What are you doing here?"

"I live here."

"I mean tonight? I thought you were in Vancouver for a week."

He came through to the living room and switched on a light. Noelle's eyes widened in alarm, she was only wearing an old cotton T-shirt for bed. It hugged her figure like a second skin and barely reached mid thigh. She dashed back to the bedroom. Putting on a pair of jeans, she dragged her fingers through her hair. Who knew what she looked like!

Walking back, she found the living room empty. She continued to the kitchen to find Linc standing by the stove, waiting for the teakettle to boil.

He looked up, his eyes dancing in amusement.

"Sorry to get you up," he said, not sounding sorry in the least. "I like your sleeping gear."

She ignored the comment. "I thought you were gone until late next week."

"Those were the plans. However, most of the men I was to see came down with the flu. Their entire office was sick. Today only two people showed up for work. Not wanting to get sick myself, I postponed the rest of the discussion until such time as they are healthy again."

"Oh."

Now what? She hadn't even searched for an apartment, thinking she'd have all weekend and then some.

"I can be out in the morning," she said.

He shrugged, turning back to the kettle just starting to whistle. "Don't move out on my account. You can stay until you find a place, if you like."

She stared at him in disbelief.

"I can't stay here. What would people think?"

"What people?" he asked, leaning against the counter.

Looking at him closely, Noelle could tell he was tired. The faint lines around his eyes looked deeper. His casual attitude seemed subdued.

"People at the office," she said.

"Betty knows you're staying here, but I doubt anyone else does. If they do, so what?"

She looked away. So what was right. It wasn't as if Linc was planning some grand seduction scene—at least not with her. No one had come right out and asked where she was staying, so who would know? Betty was the soul of discretion.

"I planned to look at some apartments this weekend," she said. "Betty gave me a new list."

"Any in this neighborhood?"

She shook her head. She wasn't sure where any of them

were, but she had obtained a map and planned to figure out the most efficient way to view all the places.

Noelle grew more conscious of Linc's closeness. When he reached into the cabinet by her, he almost brushed his arm against her shoulder. She should move, but instead remained where she was, feeling a delicious tingling as he drew near. She watched him take the coffee from the freezer and pour some beans into a grinder.

"Want any?" he asked.

"Not now. I'd never sleep."

He ground the beans, the sound loud in the quiet kitchen. Noelle realized she missed the companionship of a relationship. Did Linc?

"Why didn't you ever marry?" she asked.

He looked surprised. "We covered that before, didn't we? I've never met the right woman."

"Trevor said it was because of your parents," she said.

Why was she pursuing this topic? It was more personal than she should get with Linc Mathias.

"Because my mother walked out and my dad wasn't far behind?" he said.

She couldn't tell if the bare facts held pain after all these years. But for the young boy, it must have been devastating.

"Your grandparents loved you," she said.

"They raised me—there's a big difference. They were honorable people thrust into an untenable situation—abandon their only grandchild or put their own lives on hold and raise him. They did their best."

"But you didn't like it there."

He shook his head. Taking a sip of the hot coffee a moment later, he looked over the rim of the mug at her.

"What else did Trevor tell you?"

"That as soon as you turned eighteen and graduated, you enlisted in the Army. Got your education while in the service. Started this company when you got out."

"Succinct. Did he tell you I wanted to date you when we all started out, but I felt it would be a conflict of interest to date an employee?"

4

Noelle stared at him. "You're kidding." She felt stunned. Linc had wanted to date her?

"No. I was still debating the ethics of the situation when Trevor came in one morning and said he'd asked you out."

She swallowed hard. Her heart was pounding again. "So you backed off?"

"He was my friend. I wasn't going where he wanted to go."

"I never knew that."

What would life have been like if Linc had asked her out first? Even today she had an unruly sense of awareness whenever he was close by. She couldn't stop the images that flooded—Linc taking her out, taking her home and kissing her good-night.

Growing warm with her imagination, she tried to stay in the present.

"Actually I don't think Trevor knew, either," he said.

She wanted to ask if he still wanted to take her out, but dared not. They couldn't go back to being the two single people they'd been six years ago. She'd fallen in love with Trevor and married him. Now he was dead. But he'd always be between them.

How far had Linc's interest gone? Enough to make him leave Washington to relocate to California? Or was she giving too much importance to her role in his decisions?

"You believed I married Trevor for his money, didn't you?" she asked slowly, remembering the accusations Paul had made and Linc had never refuted.

"At the time, I wondered," he said evenly. "I thought that was why you jumped at the chance at dating a man old enough to be your father."

"I loved him."

"So it appears. He was happy with you, Noelle. Whatever your reasons were, you made him a happy man."

"You're as bad as Paul. I did *not* marry him for his money!"

She'd loved Trevor. She also had married him because of the security he offered. That was not her overriding reason, however, so she kept quiet about that aspect. She didn't want to give rise to any speculation at this late date.

"No, I'm not anything like Paul. He didn't want his brother to marry anyone. He wanted to keep control of all that family money. He and Trevor butted heads more than once about that. But it didn't change anything in the end. Trevor was as entitled to the money as Paul."

"He called again, by the way," Noelle said.

"Paul?"

"Yes. He's asking for a full accounting of money drawn down in the last year, saying Trevor wasn't in his right mind because of the tumor."

"I hope you told him to go to hell."

"I told him he was crazy and I didn't have to do it. But he's threatening to file legal actions," she said.

She was worried he'd find grounds to take back the money Trevor had saved for her. She could manage without it, but it was such a nice cushion that took the fear out of making it on her own. It was Trevor's final gift to her. She didn't want anyone questioning it.

"Let him. There are a lot of people who will affirm Trevor was in complete control of his mind right up until the end."

"He did draw down more than normal, to give me that nest egg," she said worriedly.

"I'm sure Trevor was within his rights to do that. He was so worried about you."

"Enough that he asked you to watch out for me. I'm not a baby. I don't need watching out for," she said with some heat.

She wondered if Trevor had mentioned to Linc about marrying her as he'd suggested to her before he'd died. She did sincerely hope he hadn't!

"You agreed, too," he said.

"To make him feel better."

"And what reason do you think I had?" Linc asked.

That gave her pause.

"You said yes because you also wanted to ease his last days," she said slowly. That's what friends did. And wives. "So we can negate the deal, since we both issued promises under pressure?"

He shook his head. "It doesn't work that way for me. I gave my word, I'll stick to it."

"Me, too," she said, wishing Trevor had never voiced that request. She could have stayed in D.C., found another job. Stayed away from a man who turned her upside down with just a look.

And face Paul alone? Here she had Linc at her side.

"Go back to bed, Noelle," he said. "We'll handle Paul if and when we need to."

Saturday morning Noelle slept in late. She wasn't surprised after staying up with Linc until after two. She took a quick shower, conscious he was just a few steps away. Was he still sleeping? Or had he gotten up early to take a run? He and Trevor had gone jogging together when Linc visited Washington. Noelle had never been asked.

She was still reeling from his revelation he'd wanted to ask her out. She'd had a crush on him at first, but when Trevor had started taking her to dinners and the theater, she'd realized what a special man he was. Her dealings with Linc had remained on a business footing.

How would her life have turned out if Linc had asked her first?

When she entered the kitchen, the coffee was made. She poured herself a cup, looking for a message. There was none.

She began preparing a full breakfast and was already half way through when the front door opened. A moment later Linc entered the kitchen, hair damp with perspiration, jogging clothes rumpled.

"Have a good run?" she asked.

He nodded, getting a large glass of water and drinking it down nonstop. He looked at the food on her plate. "Looks good, fix me some, would you?"

"Sure. It'll be ready by the time you're finished in the shower."

Noelle liked to cook, but breakfast wasn't a meal to showcase. Scrambled eggs, sausage and toast were pretty standard items. Someday she'd like to make an elegant breakfast of eggs Benedict or a Spanish omelet or something a bit more exciting.

She was on her second cup of coffee, his breakfast just ready to be dished up, when Linc came back wearing jeans and a polo shirt. His hair was still damp, combed away from his face.

"Thanks."

He ate without conversation, almost ignoring Noelle. She cleaned up, refreshed her coffee and sat opposite him. He looked at her.

"Ready to go apartment shopping?" he asked.

"Yes. I take it you still plan to go with me."

"I'll drive; we'll get around faster that way. Where's the first one?"

"I'll get the maps and printout."

Soon they were on their way to the first one. By mid-afternoon, Noelle had found one she liked in Pacific Heights. She and the landlord discussed terms, came to an agreement and she signed a month-to-month lease. The apartment was vacant and she could move in as soon as her furniture arrived.

"Now I have a place for the movers when they arrive,"

she said happily when they were heading back to Linc's place on Nob Hill. "In the meantime, since I can move in anytime, I'll get a bed and some furniture to supplement what I have coming. Enough to tide me over until the rest of the furnishings arrive."

"Or you can just wait until your stuff gets here. It's only another week or so, isn't it? Stay where you are until then."

Noelle didn't know what to say. Ever since he'd made mention that he'd almost asked her out on a date six years ago, she had become even more aware of Linc. Today's outing had been a strain. He'd been courteous and she'd tried not to read more into it. He'd touched her from time to time, accidentally brushing against her while viewing apartments, and she'd felt each contact like an electric shock.

How could she stay in his apartment, seeing him every day? Sharing meals, knowing he was just a few feet away when she slept?

Wondering if he still wanted to take her out.

No, she was still grieving over her husband's death. She didn't need the mix of emotions being around Linc brought.

Still, if she was to be practical, it made sense. She could eat her meals out, make sure she stayed in the bedroom when she was in the apartment. Save hotel expenses.

"Good grief, Noelle, it's not such a big deal. Just stay."

"Okay. Thanks."

She twisted her fingers in her lap, wishing she didn't find Linc so intriguing. She needed to make some friends and get a life. Maybe she should volunteer at the local animal shelter. She'd enjoyed working at the one near their home in Virginia.

Until her schedule was more fixed, however, she wasn't sure of her free time.

"Linc, I need more to do," she said as he pulled into the underground parking.

"Like what?"

"I don't know, but I'm not busy at the office. Trevor worked hard and you're always on the go. I need to do more. Trevor talked to prospective clients—I could do some of that."

"Trevor knew what we were doing, how to work up a presentation that met the client's needs. What do you know about how we operate? You've been on the administration side of things. It takes more than a week or so to learn all we offer."

"So if I do learn, could I work with clients?"

He shrugged. "Maybe."

"Then teach me."

"It would take you the better part of this year to come up to speed. Then you'll be off—"

"Not necessarily."

"What?" He had pulled the car into its slot and cut the engine.

A good thing, Noelle thought, from the stunned expression on his face.

"Maybe I'll stay with the business. I have to work somewhere. Where better than here where I'm a partner?"

"The deal was for a year."

"Trevor set that deal. We've already discussed that. He made no stipulations beyond the year. What if I don't want you to buy me out?"

Linc leaned his head back on the car seat and closed his eyes. Noelle's staying wasn't an option. He was having a hard enough time dealing with her now. Knowing she was leaving in eleven and a half months was the only thing keeping him going. How would he deal with her staying around indefinitely?

Not well.

He wanted her, but she was Trevor's widow. The man had trusted Linc to watch out for his wife and then buy her portion of the business so she'd be set for life. He couldn't betray that trust.

"It's a done deal," he said.

"So we'll change it. What if I turn out to be a wonderful salesperson? I could bring the woman's touch to things—open up a whole new division. What about targeting security for single women who live alone or even with roommates? I think that would be a more viable way to expand than to going into software development."

He opened his eyes, staring at the roof of the car. She was so enthusiastic. The company focused on foiling kidnapping, terrorist activities and other scenarios for businessmen. But there might be a market for women living alone. Maybe she was on to something.

He rolled his head and looked at her. Her eyes were shining with excitement, light pink tinged her cheeks. Her hair was tousled from the breeze outside. He wanted to run his fingers through and smooth the flyaway strands.

"There may be some merit in your idea, but I thought you were headed back to Washington after the year."

"Things change. I'm enjoying San Francisco. I have nothing back in D.C. to return to except memories that would only make me sad."

She at least kept Trevor in the forefront. He could do the same. He owed Trevor and would deliver.

"Let's discuss it more when we get upstairs," he said.

Getting out of the car, he waited for her and they walked to the elevator together.

"You'll have a tough learning curve to come up to speed quickly on our products, on how we tailor plans for individuals and corporations. We'd have to expand to local markets. Targeting individual women living alone would be a radically different aspect. We could see what we can incorporate from what we already have and what other avenues to explore."

"If I'm in on the ground floor of developing strategies for women, I'll learn as we develop. Maybe that's the direction we should take. I can't come up to speed for a while with your current standard operations. And I might not be as impressive to businessmen as a male operative would be. But I would be as knowledgeable as anyone on a new program. And a woman could sell to another woman."

"It could work."

He hated to admit it, wished he could find a way to keep her away from the business, and happy to return to Washington next summer. But it looked as if Noelle had her own plans. And they seemed to differ from those Trevor had for her.

He'd had six years to get used to treating Noelle as Trevor's. He could do it forever, he hoped.

She barely waited until they were in the apartment before she started in on her idea.

"Have you been thinking about this for a while?" he asked, going to sit on the sofa, stretching his legs out. Despite his best intentions, he couldn't keep his eyes off her. She was so pretty when she was excited. She sat beside him, almost bubbling with energy.

"Actually, yes. I spoke about it to Trevor several months ago, but he didn't think you'd be interested. I thought more about it since staying here. I never felt nervous in Trevor's house, we were so far out in the country and all. But first you insist on using the security panel, then when you came in last night you scared me to death. I was thinking how flimsy doors and windows really are. And what are we taught as kids? Nothing about security or self-defense. Seriously think about it, Linc. I think it would be a good addition to our offerings. And it's something I could really feel involved in. Like a real partner."

A real partner. Linked together for as long as the company lasted.

Trevor, what have you done? How will I resist Noelle?

"Tell you what, I have to return to Vancouver as soon as the flu has worked its way through all the principal players, so why don't you work with Sam and Howard and get some basic ideas in hand, and then we'll all discuss it when I get back. That'll give you some time to get enough of a handle on what we're doing to see what might apply to your idea."

She stared at him, almost bemused.

"What?" Wasn't he moving fast enough for her?

"Thank you, Linc. That means a lot."

He shrugged. Restless, he rose and headed for his bedroom where he kept his home computer.

"I need to check my e-mail," he said in passing. He was running, but he didn't see another choice that worked.

Noelle watched him leave, her heart thudding in her chest. He'd listened to her idea—really listened. And was giving her the okay to proceed. She almost couldn't believe it.

Trevor hadn't taken her idea seriously, simply telling her he'd look into it. But Linc was giving her free rein. Amazing.

She jumped up and hurried to her room. She needed paper and pen to jot down all her ideas. She was thrilled to be actually doing something important, rather than just processing paper.

Her only regret–she was doing it after Trevor's death. Her husband had considered his role to take care of her. She always thought it was because he was so much older and viewed life a bit differently than she did. He hadn't liked her working, but she'd convinced him she needed to do something or go crazy and why not keep her where she already knew something about the business?

But she'd never been considered partnership material by Trevor. He'd tried to keep her sheltered from the realities of life although he couldn't keep her away from the final reality—his death.

Noelle plunged into her ideas, jotting notes as random thoughts flashed into her mind. She wanted to review them with Linc, to see if he had other suggestions, but she hesitated. Would he take that as confirmation she wasn't ready to head a project? Or did the men also brainstorm ideas for new ways to protect people?

By Tuesday, Noelle was a nervous wreck. She had to move into her apartment soon because living with Linc—living in Linc's home, she corrected herself—was driving her quietly insane. Ever since he'd returned from Vancouver, she'd become more and more aware of the man. She listened for him when she was in her room, trying to guess what he was doing. They kept apart, he in his bedroom, she in the guest bedroom. But despite the walls that separated them, Noelle was attuned to his presence.

She'd hear him on the phone–and try to ignore the tingles of awareness that coursed through her. When she'd hear him in the kitchen, it was all she could do to keep from dashing there to get a glass of water or cup of tea. Forcing herself to wait until it was silent, she'd then walk down the hall for a snack. Twice she almost stopped to ask Linc if he wanted to join her. But better sense prevailed. She was trying not to see him, not to depend upon him like she had Trevor. She had her own plans, her own future to see to.

But it was hard to resist.

She looked again at the project proposal she'd written. It followed the same format as others she'd seen over the years. She was ready to present the preliminary idea to Sam and Howard. She knew it needed more work but she wanted some feedback to make sure she was on target.

She picked up the report and headed for Linc's office.

She'd update him before talking with the operatives.

"Got a minute?" she asked from the door Betty had waved her through.

He looked up. It was the first time she'd really seen him since their apartment hunting trek last Saturday. He looked tired. Was something wrong?

"A few." He tossed the pen he'd been using onto his desk and leaned back in his chair. "What's up?"

She stepped inside and put the proposal on his desk.

"I have a preliminary work-up for the idea I had and plan to discuss it with Sam and Howard. Did you want a peek first?"

She felt like a kid in school trying for an A. But it was her first major contribution—if that—and she wanted him to like it.

He glanced at the top page, then pulled the report closer and began to read. Noelle sat on one of the visitor chairs and watched him. With his concentration on the pages, she could look to her heart's content.

He looked tired. There were faint lines around his eyes she didn't remember. She wished he'd tell her if something was wrong.

His hair was dark and gleaming in the light from the windows. It looked thick. She looked away before she began fantasizing about running her fingers through it.

His hands were large and strong, with neatly trimmed nails. He turned a page. His concentration was something she found intriguing. When he focused on anything, he gave it his full attention.

She remembered how she felt when he looked at her—as if she was the only woman in the world. She swallowed, wondering what a woman in love with Linc would feel when he turned his gaze on her.

Her heart pumped a bit faster and she took a deep breath, trying to quell the excitement that raced through at the speculation.

He finished reading and looked at her. Their gazes locked and Noelle felt as if he'd physically touched her. She felt alive as never before.

"Good work," he said.

She let go the breath she hadn't realized she was holding, the warmth of his praise flooding through her.

"Thanks. It needs work, I know, but it's a start."

"A very good start. Get with the two operatives and hash it out. Once the three of you are satisfied, then plan to present it to the next staff meeting. See who wants to work on the project. I think Howard will probably stick with it, but there may be others."

She nodded, feeling almost giddy with relief. She didn't know what she'd have done if he'd thought it to be a load of trash.

"Do you see any glaring holes?" she asked, not wanting to leave just yet.

They shared an apartment, but rarely saw each other. Work was the only common ground they had. She wanted to hold on to this connection just a little longer.

"I think you should offer a few different options, to make the program flexible and more affordable to the average working woman. You can target different age groups, and focus on what they do—like the elderly who shop during the day, or young singles who go bar hopping and all. Home security is good. How about car safety or public transit awareness?"

She nodded. "I've thought of some of those, but didn't know how exactly to address the safety issue."

"Bring it up with Sam and Howard, they're old hands at this kind of thing," he said again. He looked at the report. "Good job," he said again.

She wanted him to look at her. To feel that shiver of sensation when his eyes met hers. But he picked up his pen and began to fiddle with it. It was clearly a dismissal. She smiled and rose.

"Thanks," she said.

It was as if he didn't even want to talk to her. Had she done something to offend him? Make him angry? She reviewed Saturday's outing and every day since. She could find nothing out of the ordinary.

Pausing at the door she looked back. His dark eyes were watching her. She swallowed.

"Is anything wrong?"

He shook his head slowly.

Noelle left, wishing they had built up a friendship over the years so she could talk to him more easily.

I wanted to date you. The words echoed. Did the past have any bearing on the present? What if he wanted to date her now?

She went to the ladies' lounge and splashed cold water on

her face. She wasn't ready to date anyone. She still missed her husband. At this point she knew intellectually she might move on, but emotionally she wasn't ready. She was still grieving over her loss. How could she even think about something from the long distance past? She and Linc were business partners, nothing more.

5

September

Noelle let herself into her apartment and carried the bag of groceries into the small kitchen. She had eaten dinner before stopping by the small corner store for a few items for breakfast.

She put everything away in only a couple of moments, folding the bag and stuffing it in the space between the fridge and the counter. The kitchen was immaculate. It didn't take much to feed one person, especially as she was eating lighter than normal. Except if she stopped to eat at one of the restaurants between work and the apartment.

Walking back toward the bedroom she glanced around. This was her home. The furnishings had arrived a couple of weeks ago and filled the small apartment. She missed the spaciousness of the big rambling home she and Trevor had shared, but tried not to regret the loss. She had enough to do in San Francisco to keep her focused on the future.

Reaching the small bedroom, she looked at the new queen-size bed. The one she and Trevor had shared remained in the old family home in Virginia. This was symbolic of her new life. One that was easier to deal with because she wasn't still surrounded by familiar things, she thought, shedding her business suit for more comfortable attire.

Wandering back into the living room, she sat on the love seat and gazed out the window. The view was not of tree-covered land or even a pretty view of one of the Bay Area bridges. Just another apartment building across the street.

She'd deliberately left work at the office tonight. She'd brought files and reports home with her every night since she'd moved in a week ago, to fill the evening hours.

But today she had decided she needed to get a life in San Francisco. Now that she had a home, however, she had no energy to go out to meet people or find new activities to join.

She'd noted a series of lectures at one of the library branches close to the new apartment. But she didn't feel like attending.

She had met another tenant on her floor, but only in passing. The woman was older, married, and the likelihood of their becoming friends was remote.

Being a partner in the firm wasn't any easier, either, she thought. Since technically she was the boss of almost everyone in the company, friendships at work were unlikely. Unless it was with Linc.

Which was the crux of her problem, she admitted. They had not made any overtures as friends. He was gone almost as much as he was there. After he'd returned from the curtailed Vancouver trip, he had almost immediately left for Hong Kong. He'd been back in the office two days and she'd only caught glimpses of him.

He'd been out of the country when she moved.

Not that she needed help moving, she'd had professional movers for that. But she'd hoped to have him over for dinner or something to celebrate her new independence.

And to discuss the problems Paul was causing.

Almost as if thinking about her former brother-in-law conjured him up, the phone rang. She let the answering machine pick up.

"Noelle, this is Paul. Call me. I tried you at work, but they said you were in meetings. How many meetings does a glorified secretary need? If you think avoiding my calls will change anything, you're wrong. I have an attorney preparing a request to audit funds." There was a moment of silence. "Call me," he said again and hung up.

It was the same old story, she thought. He knew, or suspected, Trevor had taken extra money those last months and he was determined to get every penny back. Maybe she should consult an attorney on her own. She felt the money was hers, but maybe she was wrong.

"Oh, Trevor." She sighed.

She no longer felt his presence. He had been dead only a few months, but everything had changed in her life. She didn't miss him with the crushing pain as she first had. Being in a different setting, a different home, doing completely different work had had the effect of separating her from the past. Everything had changed, so she wasn't constantly reminded of him by places and things they'd seen and done together.

Even her furniture was different. Her own things had been in storage for six years because they hadn't needed them for his home. She'd almost sold everything a couple of years ago rather than pay storage fees, but was glad now she'd delayed. Trevor had sat on this love seat when he'd courted her. But it wasn't tied to him like the furnishings in the old house had been.

She hoped she'd done right by moving.

Acting on impulse, she reached for the phone and called Linc. When his cell rolled over to voice mail, she tried the office.

"Mathias," he answered. He was still there. Did she know her partner or what?

"Noelle here."

"Something wrong?"

"No. Do you always assume the worst when I call?" she asked.

"You don't usually call to just talk," he said.

"This time I'm calling with an invitation. I'd like you to come to dinner on Saturday night, to celebrate my new apartment."

He hesitated.

"You'll be in town, I checked with Betty. It's just dinner, Linc."

"Very well, I accept."

She wanted more than politeness, but would take what she got.

"Come around seven, I'll fix us a special meal."

"All right, see you then."

"If not at the office," she murmured.

"What?"

"I work a few feet down the hall from you, yet I've hardly seen you at all since you returned from Hong Kong."

"I'm catching up. I'm still here reading reports."

"When you could be home working," she teased. "You need a life, Linc."

"You could be right. I'll have to see what I can do about that."

Noelle didn't like the answer. What was wrong with her? His private life was none of her concern. Still, she wished he wanted to do something with her. Maybe take her to a showing at the DeYoung Museum or invite her to go jogging with him.

Not that she needed taking care of as Trevor had thought. It's just that she would like a bit more than the cut and dried atmosphere of the office.

"You do that. See you," she said, hanging up quickly before she said something she'd later regret.

Rising, she slipped on some walking shoes and left the apartment. September was a beautiful month in San Francisco. She'd catch a cable car to the wharf and walk along with the tourists.

And get her mind off Linc Mathias and the promises her husband had extracted from them both.

Linc hung up the phone and glared at it. He was a glutton for punishment. He should have said he was busy Saturday night. In fact, why wasn't he?

Tossing down his pen, he rose and crossed to the window. Gazing out he wasn't soothed by the thoughts that jumbled in his mind. He was used to a healthy social life and he hadn't asked anyone out since Trevor's death.

He wanted to ask Noelle out.

He gave a disgusted sound and turned around. Time to head for home. He'd change and go running; burn off some of the frustrations being around her was guaranteed to bring. He'd promised his friend he'd watch out for his wife, not put the make on her. Anyway, she'd settle in soon enough, make friends, form her own interests.

He had his own interests as well. Tomorrow he'd call Zach Warren and see if he was up for a game of hand ball. Or see if Marc Hamilton wanted to go rock climbing at Yosemite this weekend.

No, he'd promised dinner with Noelle on Saturday.

What would they talk about? Business? Trevor? Paul? Was the man still giving her trouble, or had he ended that nonsense? He'd have to check with his hostess when he got there.

Noelle with the pretty blue eyes, the excitement over the new division of women's security, the silky golden-brown hair, and radiant smile.

He punched the elevator button with more force than necessary. Running would clear his mind and give him some peace. And then maybe he'd call a woman or two he knew and ask them out. It was definitely more than time to get back in the dating scene. Trevor's death had hit him hard, but life moved on.

When would Noelle move on?

Noelle was looking forward to dinner on Saturday. It would be the first entertaining she'd do in her new home, but not the last. She and Trevor had enjoyed having friends in for dinner or meeting them at elegant restaurants around the District. She knew San Francisco was renowned for its great restaurants. She hoped she could sample all the different ethnic places and settle on some favorites.

In the meantime, she was cultivating the friendship of the owners of the small grocery store near her apartment. The neighborhood was friendly and she hoped to feel like she fit in before long.

Saturday she shopped for the freshest produce. She planned a special meal of beef burgundy over wild rice, steamed vegetables and a fresh garden salad. For dessert she was making a rich chocolate cake. She had loved to bake in the old kitchen in Virginia. This would be her first venture back since Trevor's death.

As the afternoon wore on, Noelle grew more and more sad. Trevor had loved her chocolate cake. She remembered how he'd come in when he'd smell it baking and sit with her while she frosted the layers, stealing a swipe of chocolate frosting from time to time when he thought she wasn't looking.

The dinner had been one of his favorites. Was that why she was preparing it again? Or was it because it was a proven hit with men? She wanted Linc to enjoy the dinner, after all.

But she missed Trevor and felt his loss afresh. Before long she was quietly crying.

Rushing around later, she took another shower and put cold cloths on her swollen eyes. How awful to have Linc show up and have the hostess look as if she regretted her invitation!

Applying makeup, she tried to minimize the evidence of her tears. The soft pink dress floated around her, draping her figure and making her feel feminine. It was a far cry from the more tailored outfits she wore to work and she hoped Linc would like it.

If he even noticed. He rarely seemed to look at her at work, being much too focused on business.

But tonight wasn't about business, but about two people sharing a meal and her celebrating her new home.

The buzzer startled her–its raucous sound unfamiliar. They'd had chimes in Virginia. She went to the door. Linc almost took away her breath he looked so right standing there, tall, dressed casually in dark pants and a sports coat, with his shirt unbuttoned at the throat. In his hand he held a small bouquet of flowers.

"Hi," she said, smiling in welcome.

"What's wrong?" he asked immediately.

Darn it, she hadn't camouflaged her crying jag as she'd hoped.

"Nothing. You're right on time, come in."

She stood aside to let him in.

He entered, closing the door and gently tracing the swollen skin near her eyes with his free hand.

"You've been crying? Is this too much? Should I come another time?"

"Of course not. I was missing Trevor today. He'll never see this place and he won't be here for any dinners I prepare. He won't ever know if I make a success of things at work. It's hard."

She stopped, afraid she'd start crying again for all she'd lost.

He pulled her into a warm hug, resting his chin on the top of her head. "I miss him, too. I still can't believe he's not a phone call away."

She nodded, feeling comforted, secure. Maybe she just needed to know someone else loved Trevor and missed him.

Or maybe she wanted to be held by Linc Mathias. To feel his solid strength shelter her from the world for just a moment. To imagine she'd always feel as safe as she did right now.

He couldn't change the past, but he could buffet the hardships of the future.

Stunned at the train of her thoughts, she pulled away.

"You okay now?" he asked.

Nodding she smiled brightly.

"These are for you," Linc said, holding out the flowers.

"They're so pretty, thank you."

It was a small mix bouquet of flowers—daisies, tiger lilies, baby's breath and a few peppermint carnations. She hadn't received a casual bunch like this before. Trevor had always given her long-stemmed roses for special occasions. They'd been very elegant but Noelle loved this bright mix of colors and scents.

"I'll put them in water and then in the center of the dining room table. They'll brighten things up."

"Can I help with dinner or anything?" Linc asked as she went into the small kitchen. He followed her to the doorway.

"Not a thing and, as you can see, this room isn't really big enough for two to be wandering around." Noelle made quick work of finding a vase and filling it with water. She arranged the flowers to her satisfaction and turned to go to the dining area. It was an alcove off the living room, barely large enough for a table with four chairs. Two places had been set. The flowers looked perfect.

"Something smells good," Linc said.

"I hope you like it. It'll be ready in a few minutes. Want to have a glass of wine?"

In less than ten minutes, Noelle had poured the wine and served the dinner. She wanted to begin eating right away lest she struggle for conversation.

She felt more awkward around Linc than she expected. Was it because she was entertaining alone after years being part of a couple? Or was it Linc himself?

She couldn't fight the attraction that flared whenever she was around him, but doing her best to ignore it, she fumbled for a topic of conversation.

"Tell me how you met Trevor," she said finally.

He glanced at her. "Didn't he say?"

She shrugged. "He gave an abbreviated version. Tell me your side."

Linc took another bite of food, chewed it while looking at her. "This is delicious," he said.

"Thank you." Noelle waited patiently.

"It was ten years ago," he began. "I was getting out of the service, using up the last of my leave seeing the sights in Washington. One night I was walking around near the Kennedy Center, just as some event was getting out. Trevor was heading for his car when a bunch of punks came out of the dark and tried to mug him. He fought back and I stepped in."

Linc almost smiled, his dark eyes warm with memory. "We whipped them good, then turned to each other when the last guy ran and shook hands. He thanked me for my help. I said he fought pretty good for a civilian."

"He told me that, but he always thought you substituted civilian for old man," she said.

Hearing Linc tell the tale sent shivers down her back. Both men were lucky to have walked away unscathed.

"No, I meant it. It was dark, I didn't know how old he was then. Not that it mattered. Trevor never seemed old, you know what I mean?"

"Yes, I do. Go on."

"He offered to give me a ride back to the base. It was late, so I accepted. One thing led to another and we got together a week later for lunch. He asked what I planned to do when I got out of the service. I told him my idea to start up a firm teaching people how to stay safe under dangerous circumstances. Then he laughed— 'Like I ran into coming from the Kennedy Center last week?' he said."

"So you two started Simpson and Mathias," she finished.

"Not right away. Is that what he said?"

She nodded. "I said it was an abridged version. What happened next?"

"He gave me his card and told me to call him if I was serious. Having had enough orders in the military, I was noncommittal, but planned to make it on my own. It was only after I made a start, and realized after a year or so how much I needed more capital and more advice, that I called Trevor. We had only been in business together a year or so when you started work there."

"You had already started the company before Trevor joined?" Noelle hadn't known that.

"A small firm offering security services to those living in Washington. You know all the embassies there. I started small, showing those new to D.C. how to get proper security in their homes and cars, what to watch for when shopping or going downtown late at night. But I wanted to do more. Trevor's infusion of capital enabled me to implement more of the ideas I had. If I'd waited until I could have afforded to expand on my own, I would still be offering basic services to Washingtonians."

"Instead the firm has grown until it now employs over fifty people and is world-wide in scope. Amazing."

"Thanks to Trevor," Linc said.

He filled their glasses again before meeting her eyes.

He told her about the early days, the difficulties they overcame, the new directions they started. Some aborted attempts to expand. And how their most recent expansion seemed to be doing well.

"But he offered more than money. That enabled us to get up and running, but it was his friendship I valued more," Linc finished.

She nodded. "He knew it. He hated your moving from Washington."

Linc took a sip of wine, glancing at the empty plates on

the table, at the vase of flowers. Elsewhere, but not at Noelle.

She knew now why he'd gone and suddenly felt guilty for keeping the two friends apart. But there was nothing she could have done differently. Linc had made his choices and they'd all had to live with them.

"I hope you saved room for dessert," she said, rising.

She gathered their plates and went to the kitchen. Putting the dishes in the sink, she ran water on them, hoping to regain her equilibrium. She'd enjoyed hearing Linc talk about Trevor, and about their early days together before she'd joined the company. Not only had they started a good firm, they'd had fun doing it.

She carried the cake to the table. A second trip brought plates and forks and a knife. As she sliced the cake, she glanced at Linc. Her heart sped up when her eyes met his.

"Thank you for talking about Trevor. Sometimes it's almost as if he didn't exist. I'm the only one around here, besides you, who really knew him. The only one affected by his being gone. Maybe I should have stayed in Washington. At least there I had mutual friends."

"I miss him more than you know," Linc said quietly.

She handed him a plate with cake and took one for herself.

"Paul giving you any more trouble?" he asked.

She shrugged. "He had an attorney contact me about illegal use of funds. I turned the letter over to an attorney Betty recommended, Hamilton Smythe? Apparently you used him for some small case and thought him competent."

"He is. Did he think there was any merit in the letter?"

"No. He did, however, suggest I do something with the

money, besides letting it just sit in a bank account. Maybe I should invest it in our company."

"No need. You already own half the shares."

"But that was inherited. I'd feel more a part of things if I put something in."

"Invest it in bonds or something safe. The company is starting to show profits on the Pacific Rim expansion, but nothing is a sure thing."

"I think working with you is," she said, meeting his eyes. "Thank you for giving me a chance with my idea."

"Looks like you have another winner. We'll be expanding all over," he said.

After dessert, she prepared coffee and they moved to the living room. Noelle put on a CD of soft jazz. From her memory of Linc's collection, she thought he'd enjoy it.

"So are you all settled?" Linc asked, glancing around.

She'd put some much-loved paintings on the walls, a few photographs of her and Trevor on the side table. The rest of the room was rather austere, but he liked the feeling of space and simplicity. The home he'd visited in Virginia had been crammed with antiques and knickknacks—many from Trevor's mother.

Was this more Noelle's style? He'd never thought about her moving into Trevor's house and living with his things. Didn't most women want to start fresh and make their own mark when nesting?

"I'm all settled, even have extra space in the bookcase in the room I'm using as an office. Want the grand tour?" she asked.

He'd seen the apartment when they'd been searching for a place, but not with her furniture in it.

"Sure."

He rose, following her down the short hall to the smaller of the two bedrooms. She'd set up a desk with a laptop computer. The window overlooked the street, but it wasn't much of a view. He noticed the partially empty bookcase and the small TV on a rolling stand.

"I'm trying not to use this for work," she said with a smile.

He expected her to start making friends and doing things outside of work. Most people didn't spend as much time in the office as he did.

"Bath," she said back in the hall, pointing to an opened door.

He peeked in, taking note of the feminine things scattered on the counter. Perfume bottles, a brush, and a basket with lipsticks. How many different colors did a woman need, he wondered, glancing back at her lips. They appeared soft and faintly pink.

Desire hit hard and low. He wanted to taste those lips, feel their softness against his own. See if kissing her would be as wonderful as he'd always imagined.

"My bedroom is here," she said, walking to another opened door.

Linc stepped up and looked into the room. He'd expected lace and pillows, and instead found another soothing room simplistic in design. Cool colors of blue and turquoise highlighted the room. The white curtains on the windows added to the cool tone. He'd like to wake up in a room like that–with Noelle.

Turning, he headed back to the living room. He needed to get out while he could, before he said or did something unforgivable. He'd done his duty coming to dinner. The meal was finished, so now he could leave.

"Thanks for the tour," he said, looking at his watch. "I need to go."

"Go? It's early. I thought we could talk some more," she said, looking startled with his announcement.

"We talk all the time. What more do you want to discuss?"

"Nothing in particular."

She looked flustered.

Linc wanted to pull her into his arms again, as he had when he'd first arrived. Not, this time, for comfort, however. He wanted to feel her softness, smell the sweet scent that emanated from her. To kiss her and feel her passion rise and respond to his. Have her cling to him as she must have done with Trevor.

Trevor.

Blast it, he'd been his best friend. What was he *thinking?*

Leave, that's what he had to do.

"I just thought you might stay longer, that's all," she said. "If you have to go, okay. Thanks for coming, and for the flowers."

"Dinner was delicious," he said.

She reached out and rubbed her fingertips along his sleeve. "I'm glad you came."

He reacted to her touch instantly. Pulling her gently into his arms, he slowly lowered his head and found her mouth, kissing her like the world was ending tomorrow. Her lips were as soft as they looked, and warm. She tasted sweeter than the chocolate cake they'd shared earlier. The heat that enveloped them seemed to sear through to his heart.

Noelle didn't push him away.

She didn't respond, either.

Linc pulled back and looked into her eyes, seeing the uncertainty, the wariness.

"That was a mistake," he forced the words out.

"Was it?" she asked softly.

Her fingertip traced his lower lip.

"It was unexpected, but I'm not sure it was a mistake," she said softly gazing back into his eyes.

He accepted the invitation and kissed her again. As the sensations rose, he was conscious of every bit of her pressed to him, of the response he dreamed about for years being freely given. Of the taste of her, the heat, the desire.

Take care of Noelle for me. The thought crashed into his mind with the force of a sledgehammer.

Linc eased her away and yanked open the door. Leaving before he made the biggest mistake of his life.

6

Noelle stood completely still. She felt the sweeping sensations of Linc's kiss. The heat that had spiraled through her dissipated slowly as she listened to the door slam shut. The carpet in the hallway muffled Linc's steps, but she knew they'd be long and fast.

Kiss and run.

Just like a man, she thought with exasperation. She went to the door and locked it, keying in her security code absently.

She wasn't sure she wanted him to kiss her. The emotions that flooded through her were a mixture of curiosity, guilt and latent desire. Hadn't she been interested in the man all those years ago before Trevor had swept her off her feet? And wasn't she totally aware of him on a physical level anytime he came near her?

So why wouldn't she be curious? She'd wondered about kissing him and now she had.

And wow, what a kiss.

She gathered the coffee cups and headed for the kitchen. Maybe doing such mundane chores like washing the dishes would gain her some perspective.

Her heart continued to beat rapidly. Her mouth pulsed with the feel of Linc's. Licking her lips, she could taste him and her heart rate kicked up another notch.

Then guilt took over, smothering the desire.

Trevor had been dead less than four months and she was already kissing another man? How could she? She'd loved her husband and she missed him desperately.

That was it, she was desperately lonely and giving into the first man who came along.

Noelle laughed. The notion that Linc was a substitute for her husband was ludicrous. He was too virile to be a substitute for anyone.

Her reaction scared her a little. She should be thinking of Trevor, not Linc. She did miss her husband, though not as much as she thought she would at this stage. Had she begun some of her grieving before he'd even died?

They'd had weeks to prepare for his death. Closure, she thought. They'd said all they wanted, talked of their happy lives together. He'd made her promise to look forward and not back. And let Linc take care of her.

Moving out of their home had been the first tie severed.

The transfer to San Francisco had changed everything. She had none of her close friends around to help—or to keep Trevor's memory in the forefront. She knew she had to move on. She was doing her best, as she had promised her husband she would.

Noelle turned off the kitchen light. Had Linc been thinking of that promise when he kissed her? She hoped not. She wanted to believe he kissed her because he wanted to, not as some kind of convoluted promise to his friend to take care of her.

Linc drove into the parking garage and pulled into his space. In only moments he was in the elevator for the office. He could always lose himself in work. The contingent in Vancouver had recovered, so he could finalize plans to make that trip again. And he wanted to review Noelle's plans with Harvey, hoping Harvey would be able to act as the sounding board on new ideas. They should discuss hiring more female operatives who could relate to the women clients they were now wooing.

His office was dark, lit only by the light from other buildings. No one worked on Saturday nights, he thought as he flipped on the overhead lights and moved to the desk. No one but a man trying to forget an armful of femininity that had his blood heating up like nothing ever had before.

Take care of Noelle, Trevor had asked. Not make a move on my wife.

Widow, Linc corrected.

He sat behind his desk but didn't touch the stacks of paper. Instead, he leaned back and considered the situation. He'd been intrigued with Noelle since the first day she joined the firm. There was no use speculating on what might have happened if he'd asked her out that first day. Years had gone by.

He'd opened the west coast office, expanded the company, trained operatives and developed new techniques to keep people safe in these unsafe times. Nothing was the same as it had been six years ago.

What would happen if he asked her out now?

He frowned. Trevor hadn't been dead six months yet. It

was too early for Noelle to be interested in another man. Heck, she might never be interested in him.

But he wanted to be right there when she began to date again. He wouldn't wait around this time–instead he'd be the first man to take her out—when she was ready.

How would he know that? From her response to his kiss, he might think she was ready now. But wasn't it too soon? Did he have the patience to wait?

He sat up and pulled a thick folder over, opening it. He had work to do. When the time was right, he'd trust his instincts. Until then he hoped his patience would hold.

Noelle entered the office Monday morning with some trepidation. She wasn't sure what to say to Linc when she saw him. Should she ignore their kiss? She hadn't been able to do so during the weekend. That memory had dominated her thoughts all day Sunday, and was at the forefront of her mind right now.

"Good morning," Harvey greeted her as she passed him in the hall. "Got a sec?"

"Good morning. What's up?"

"If you have time this morning, Linc wanted you to bring me up to speed on the new direction you're going with the women's safety program. I'd like to get as much info as I can before he gets back."

"Gets back?"

"He left for Vancouver earlier this morning."

Noelle hadn't known he was leaving. Had he said

something that she missed Saturday night? No, she would have remembered.

Had he made these plans after dinner at her place?

"Let me put my things down and check my calendar. As soon as I have some free time, we can review what I have," she said, a bit miffed Linc had gone without a word to her.

And that he was assigning others to her project without her input. She wasn't sure Harvey Winters was the man she wanted backing her. She rather thought a promotion for Betty would work better.

She called Betty when she reached her desk.

"Where's Linc?"

"He left for Vancouver. He's going to meet with that group that got sick when he was up there before."

"Is he calling in?" Noelle asked.

"I'm sure he will. Do you need me to reach him? He's at the airport now. The flight doesn't take off until ten."

"I have his cell number, I'll call him."

Noelle closed her door and punched in the numbers for his cell phone.

"Mathias," his deep voice responded.

"Noelle here," she said, annoyed to feel the involuntary quickening of her heart at the sound of his voice.

"Problems?" he asked.

"I thought we were partners. When you gave the okay for me to develop a line of security features and training for women, I expected to be treated as an equal. You have the direction of the company in mind, but I have certain expectations in this particular line and want to do what I want."

"And that is a problem how?"

"Harvey."

"You don't want him working with you?"

"I should have been consulted. Actually I planned to talk to you about promoting Betty to help me with this. I think we would show more confidence in our product and services with women showing other women how to stay safe than we would having some man in confusing the issue."

"Confusing the issue," he repeated slowly.

"I don't want clients to think the training and equipment is only viable because some guy is involved."

"Ah. It is my company and I'm a guy."

"It's our company and I'm not."

"I know that," he muttered.

She gripped the phone harder. Should she say something about the kiss? Or had it been only a moment's aberration, quickly forgotten? She didn't want to make more of it than it warranted. To her it was a big deal. To a man like Linc it probably was one in a long line.

"Look, Noelle, if you feel Betty is the better choice, tell Harvey. But I think you could actually use them both and hire a few more people as this project takes off. I don't want to pull staff from other projects, so we'll be expanding here. Get who you think you need. Have Harvey be the in-house resource. If Betty takes the job, train her in the security methods and have her be one of your reps. This is your baby, you handle it as you see fit."

"Thank you," she said, warmed at the confidence he apparently had in her. Trevor had pooh-poohed the entire idea. Linc let her take the idea and run with it—as she saw fit.

"How long are you planning to be in Vancouver?" she asked.

"A few days. Don't take my secretary without getting me another one," he said.

"We'll manage here while you're gone. A sudden trip, isn't it?"

The hesitation on the other end told her what she wanted to know—he wasn't as immune to their kiss as she'd thought.

"Should have been done earlier, but they all got sick, remember?"

"I do. Have a good flight. Bring home a huge contract," she said, feeling lighter than she had when she arrived at work.

October

It was late by the time Noelle left the office. The last six weeks had been so hectic, she sometimes didn't know which way was up. But she felt alive as she never had before.

The new branch of women's security was already showing sales. After polishing and fine-tuning their offerings, they'd done informational seminars to as many women's groups as they could book over the last two weeks and orders were pouring in.

She'd hired two women with police backgrounds to work with Betty, who had been delighted with the promotion. They'd all come up to speed together–driven by Harvey Winters, who turned out to be a drill sergeant in disguise.

He'd pushed and yelled at them all until they were as

proficient in the various techniques of defense as they could be on such short training. Contrary to her initial reaction, Noelle recognized a team player when she saw one and now considered Harvey a valued member of their team.

Of Linc she'd seen very little. He was still traveling more than she'd expected, only in the office a day or two at a time and then gone again. Their dinner had been forgotten. And only sometimes just before she fell asleep at night did she think of that kiss.

He'd finished the presentation in Vancouver, getting the contract they'd angled for. A couple of days in the office and he'd been off to Brussels, stopping in Washington on his way back. Another day in the office and he'd left for the Far East, with stops in Hong Kong and Tokyo as well as some down time in Hawaii.

Noelle hadn't even thought about taking a vacation. She'd taken time off with Trevor's last illness, but with the new line she was in charge of she had too much to do to consider taking a few days off. So she wasn't jealous of Linc's time in Hawaii—except to wonder who he was spending it with.

Betty appeared in the doorway, her eyes wide. She'd hired her own replacement, though she still helped out as Pam came up to speed with running Linc's office.

"Noelle, there're two detectives here to see you," she said.

"Show them in."

They'd had several calls from various precincts in the city asking about their new program. They had printed brochures that were available to anyone who wanted them. She hoped to eventually offer an overview to all law enforcement agencies interested, but they already had a backlog from the seminars of the last couple of weeks.

The two men entered, both wearing dark suits. Noelle smiled and rose, offering her hand.

"I'm Noelle Simpson. What can I do for you?"

One man flipped open a notebook. "You are the widow of Trevor Simpson of Leesburg, Virginia?"

She realized this was probably not going to be a request to discuss the company's new services.

"That's right. Please, have a seat."

She sat quickly, her knees suddenly weak.

"What's this about?"

The second man pulled out a folded sheet of paper from his pocket and opened it, handing it to her, printed side out.

"Do you know anything about the items of jewelry listed here?"

Noelle took the sheet and scanned it. Her jewelry was listed. Not every piece, but the more valuable items Trevor had given her over the years.

"These are mine," she said quietly. She had a complete list with her insurance papers, but she recognized the descriptions.

"Can you prove ownership?" the first detective asked.

"I don't know how to prove ownership beyond saying my husband gave me these for various special occasions. They've been insured on our account for years. How does any woman prove ownership of gifts from her husband?" Noelle asked.

The men looked at each other.

"Paul wants them back, doesn't he?" she asked.

"Paul Simpson reported them missing from the family vault and suggested you might know where they were," one said carefully.

"They aren't missing, they were gifts to me from my husband," Noelle reiterated. "He was Paul's brother. Trevor is dead and Paul is trying to recover every dime my husband spent from their family trust. But Trevor did nothing wrong. He was as entitled to use the money and property as Paul. Does *his* wife have to show ownership of the jewelry he's given her over the years?"

Noelle was getting more than tired of Paul and his subtle harassment. She needed to find a way to stop him. How dare he imply she'd stolen the jewelry.

She rose. "I have nothing further to say. You may tell Paul I can account for the jewelry and I intend to keep every item. As gifts from my late husband, the pieces mean a great deal to me."

"He claims the items were missing, possibly stolen," the detective said.

"Then he'd better file a report. And then I'll sue him from one end of the country to the next for harassment and defamation. I did *not* steal anything. My husband gave me these items and I have no intention of giving them up to his brother now that he's dead."

"Is there a problem?" Linc asked, standing in the doorway.

Betty hovered just behind him.

The detectives rose and turned. "You are?" one of them asked.

"Lincoln Mathias, Noelle's business partner. What seems to be the problem?"

"Paul is accusing me of theft," Noelle said, so angry she was surprised her voice didn't waver. "He says I stole some of the Simpson family jewelry." She snatched up the listing and held it out.

Linc walked over and took it, looking at the items listed.

"Before his death, Trevor Simpson was my partner in this firm. His wife inherited his shares when he died. Trevor was also my friend," Linc said, handing the paper back to the detective. "He often told me of special surprises he had for Noelle. I remember the diamond earrings." He looked at Noelle. "For your fifth wedding anniversary, I think."

She nodded.

"Just trying to get the facts of the matter," the detective said.

"I think if you have the police in Washington check, you'll find that Noelle did not have access to the Simpson family accounts or vault. Any item taken from there had to be taken by Trevor or Paul. If a man wishes to give his wife a present, he's entitled."

"That changes things a bit," one of the detectives said, glancing at his partner.

"Maybe," said the other. "We know where to find you if we need to talk to you again," he said to Noelle.

They left and Linc thanked Betty for getting him before he closed the office door.

"I am so angry I could spit!" Noelle said, pacing from behind her desk. "How dare Paul accuse me of stealing anything! Trevor gave me every one of those pieces of his own free will. The necklace was the last thing he gave me. He knew by then his days were numbered and he felt I could sell it if I needed quick cash. But I won't. I cherish everything he gave me. And neither will I meekly return the pieces to Paul!"

Linc leaned against the door, watching her pace the small office.

"I know he gave you some of those and if you said he gave you all, I believe you. Check with your attorney again. It may be that some of the jewelry wasn't Trevor's to give away, but was on loan. If that's the slant Paul's taking, you should be prepared to deal with it."

She stopped and glared at Linc. "Whose side are you on?"

"Yours, always," he said softly.

She resumed pacing. "I'm so mad at Paul. Why can't he leave me alone? I have nothing for him."

"I always thought the man had a fanatical interest in things, rather than family. He seems to want everything Trevor ever took, money or jewelry, returned to the family trust. You need to consult with your attorney again to see how much he really is entitled to have returned, if anything," Linc advised.

"Trevor wouldn't have given me something if he hadn't been sure it was within the scope of the trust. He knew Paul didn't like me. He would have protected me," she insisted.

"I believe you, but it won't hurt to double check."

She stopped pacing and looked at him. "I didn't know you were back."

"I barely walked in before Betty told me to get over here

because there was an emergency. Seems to me you were handling it fine without me."

"Maybe. Thanks for running to the rescue."

He didn't respond. Noelle looked at him. New lines bracketed his mouth. He looked tired.

"You should go home and get some rest," she said. She could study him all day, and never get tired of it.

She moved back behind her desk.

"I thought I'd catch up with the mail, first," he said.

"You have been gone a while."

Five weeks and two days, but who was counting? Except for those brief forays into the office between trips, he'd been out of the country most of that time.

"I always travel a lot."

Linc turned and opened the door. He paused and looked back at her. "Aside from visits from the cops, how are you doing?"

"Fine. When you're caught up, we can have a discussion of the women's division. I think you'll be pleased with the grounds we've covered."

Linc nodded and headed for his own office. He almost proposed she tell him now what she'd been doing, and not only at work. He wanted to know every aspect about her life. Did she like living in San Francisco? What did she do in her time off?

And especially, was she making friends?

He'd promised Trevor he'd watch out for Noelle. He'd backed away after that kiss but a commitment was made and he'd honor it.

And dreaming about another kiss or even more had nothing to do with things. Not yet, anyway.

Linc sat behind his desk a moment later, looking at the neat stacks of mail, reports and folders his new secretary had placed on the surface. He'd closed the door and now took advantage of the silence to lean back in the chair. He was tired. A result of trying to keep unwanted thoughts at bay. The only way he found was to push himself. Nights were the hardest. If he wasn't dog-tired when he fell into bed, he'd remember. Memories of Noelle's sweet scent, her soft skin, the feel of her lips against his drove him crazy.

He had to decide—take advantage of her while she was still vulnerable from Trevor's death to push for a closer relationship. Or do the honorable thing and leave her alone.

The recent trip had been his attempt to leave her alone. Out of sight, out of mind. Only it hadn't worked that way. He could sit at dinner in a crowded restaurant and picture her sitting next to him. Be riding in a cab through a busy city street and imagine her making comments about the scenery.

He closed his eyes in frustration. He had it bad. He pulled his phone closer and looked up a number.

"Salina? Linc Mathias. How have you been?…I've been out of town lately, but I'm back for a while. Which leads me to my call, are you available for dinner Saturday night?"

Time to get his life back on track, find some female companionship and stop thinking about his partner's widow all the time.

Noelle took a long time to calm down from the visit by the police. She wanted to have a cool head when speaking with her attorney. Though at one point, she actually lifted the phone to call Paul and tell him to stop bothering her. But her rational mind took over and she resisted.

By late afternoon she'd spoken with Mr. Smythe directly. He had been Trevor's attorney and was familiar with the Simpson Family Trust. He assured her he'd reexamine it to see if there were anything Noelle should be concerned about. He reassured her that his initial take on the situation was that her husband had known the ins and outs and would never have put her in an awkward situation.

Before leaving for home, she tidied her desk. Staring out the window, she looked at the lights on nearby offices gleaming in the growing twilight. The days were getting shorter, the evenings colder. Soon she'd be leaving work in the dark. In fact, if she didn't leave soon today it'd be dark.

Still, she hesitated. It wasn't that she didn't like her apartment. It was fine. Not quite home yet, but she'd feel at home eventually.

The problem was loneliness. That was the reason she didn't want to leave.

Most of the staff had left for the day, but she could hear some muted conversations down the hall. Even though she wasn't a part of the group, she didn't feel so alone here.

Was Linc still working? He had a lot to catch up on. Betty was still doing some of his work while Pam was being trained. Linc received updates daily when he traveled.

Still, there'd been stacks of things on his desk when she passed by earlier. He'd been in meetings all day and she bet he was still catching up.

She reached for her purse and glanced around. She was beginning to fit in with the San Francisco office. The main office, now that they'd closed the one in Washington. It gave her a sense of purpose and a feeling of belonging.

Noelle walked to Linc's office. The door was ajar, but the light was off. He must have left already. She felt a wave of disappointment. She'd hoped to catch him before he left. To what end? Dinner? Some time together?

Another kiss?

The thought came unbidden, and surprised her. She'd tried to forget that kiss and had no business dreaming about her partner now. She'd been married, loved her husband and was now alone. Maybe someday she'd find someone else to make a life with.

She decided to walk home. It was growing dark, but there were plenty of people on the sidewalk and she could use the exercise and the diversion. Before long she was climbing one of the steep hills that dotted the city. There were fewer people on the sidewalk now. She was alone on her side of the block, but she wasn't worried. It was a safe neighborhood and she'd be home before long. She only had another couple of blocks of hill before she turned off and had level walking again. Not like if she went to Linc's place on the top of Nob Hill. That would be a hike and a half.

Her apartment was nothing like Linc's. His was cool, modern, contemporary. Now that her furniture had arrived, hers was more eclectic and homey. She missed some of the antiques from the rooms in the Virginia home, but not as much as she had thought she would. Maybe she'd scour antique shops in San Francisco to see what she could pick up.

For the time being, her secondhand items suited her. It wasn't as if she was entertaining or trying to impress people. They'd entertained a lot in Virginia. But not with her own friends, more with Trevor's. The couples had usually been one or two decades older than she, with their children grown. She hadn't noticed so much at the time, but thinking back, she remembered rarely having her own friends over. If they had a large pool party in summer, she'd included them. Her friend Marian especially enjoyed those parties. She had a terrific figure and said she loved having all the men watching but not touching.

Maybe she'd give Marian a call tonight. She was feeling moody and lonely and hearing from her friend would be just the thing to cheer her up. It had been several weeks since they'd caught up on gossip.

Or she could call Linc.

Her heart tripped at the thought. He wouldn't need to talk to her tonight, he could have seen her all day. Just because he was now back in the same city she was didn't mean she needed to interact with him.

But the thought wouldn't go away. When she reached her apartment, she dropped her purse and went to the phone. Punching in Linc's number, she waited with impatience.

The phone rang a half dozen times before being answered.

"Mathias," he said.

His deep, sexy voice sent shivers down her spine.

"Hi," Noelle said. "You cut out from work earlier than I expected."

"Sorry, did you need something? I got home and crashed. The time change and all."

She'd woken him. Now she felt stupid. "I'm sorry, it's nothing important. Go back to sleep. I'll catch you in the morning."

"I'm awake now."

"It's nothing."

Her mind went blank. It literally was nothing. She'd called just to talk and to take the edge off being alone in her apartment.

"See you tomorrow." She hung up, berating herself for acting like a schoolgirl in the throes of a crush on some boy.

The phone rang. Resigned, she lifted the receiver.

"Hi."

"How is the new project going?" Linc asked.

"Great. Haven't you been reading my updates?"

"Yeah, I read them. Tell me more than bland statistics."

"They aren't bland! We're really taking off."

Noelle sat on the sofa, kicked off her shoes and spoke with enthusiasm of the project.

When she wound down several minutes later, she noted he hadn't said much. "You still there?" she asked.

"Um. Good work."

"Really, Linc, you need your sleep. I can tell you're tired or you would have nitpicked something."

"I do not nitpick," he objected.

She laughed, happy to hear him. "Okay, then you would have found something to challenge."

"No, I think you have all the bases covered."

"Thank you."

She wanted to hear all he'd been doing while he'd been gone. What the new prospects were, how would that change things in the overall financial plan. But she knew he had to be exhausted.

"I have to go now–so you can get back to sleep. Thanks for listening."

"Anytime, Noelle, you know that."

She hung up reluctantly, wishing they could have had longer on the phone. She knew Linc was watching out for her. Sure he'd make time for Trevor's widow.

Sighing softly, she rose and went to change into comfy sweats. She'd fix a light meal and see if that mystery she was reading could hold her interest.

Several hours later Noelle became vaguely aware of sirens sounding. She snuggled down, turning over—and almost fell off the sofa. Sitting up, she looked around. She'd fallen asleep reading. Before she could think about getting up to go change and go to bed, there were thudding steps in the hall. A moment later someone pounded on her door.

"Fire department, anyone inside?" He pounded again.

She hurried to the door and opened it. A man in full fire turnout gear stood before her, his helmet gleaming in the hall light.

"Fire on the upper stories, you need to get out. Anyone else in the apartment?"

"No, I live alone. I'll get—"

"Nothing. You have to evacuate immediately. Move, move, move."

"My purse, then, that's all."

She reached back and nabbed it and then was hurried down the hall. The man slapped a large sticker on her door and shut it. She saw other fire department personnel at other doors, almost pushing the occupants out into the hall, all toward the stairs. It was a strange scene. Fear clogged her. She glanced overhead as if she could see fire, but everything looked normal.

Heart racing, Noelle joined two of her neighbors in hurrying down the stairs. The fire department personnel had closed the elevator. She could hear another siren coming closer, muffled slightly by the hollow-sounding echos on the cement stairs.

Reaching the ground floor, they exited to the street. She hurried into the cool night air wishing she'd picked up a jacket as well as her purse. Others from the apartment building were gathered across the street looking at their building. Most of them were wearing pajamas and robes. She joined them, seeing for the first time the flames coming from upper floor windows that lit up the night.

A woman near her was sobbing. An older couple looked on, hopelessly. Noelle glanced back. Was the blaze growing? People continued to stream from the building. She hoped no one was in the apartment that was burning and shivered, mesmerized by the flames.

The hoses began to pour water to the upper reaches. Glass shattered and shards rained down onto the sidewalk in front of the building. The fire was spreading. More trucks arrived and lines were established. Their group was pushed farther away to get out of the way of the firefighters.

"Everything I own is in there," one woman said.

"Same here," another replied.

"How did it start?" someone asked.

No one seemed to know.

Water was splashing everywhere, the street was soon glistening with it. Still the flames seemed to flare and spread.

The fight went on for a long time. Noelle didn't realize she was shivering with cold until her teeth began to chatter. She'd been watching, hoping the fire would soon be extinguished, then wondering if it would be before it consumed the entire building.

At long last it began to grow darker. The flames weren't as bright. Men and equipment were everywhere, and finally their teamwork was paying off. The fire was beaten back.

It looked as if two-thirds of the building had been involved. Broken windows looked like vacant eyes. Even the floors not touched by the fire had been damaged by smoke and water.

"We've arranged for you folks to be taken to one of the local high schools. They have emergency arrangements for large groups. Everything will get sorted out there. The bus is here. Follow me," one of the firefighters instructed their group.

Docilely they all followed to a city bus and climbed aboard. Noelle looked over her shoulder as she got on; her apartment looked as if it had escaped the flames—but not the water damage. How soon before she could return to assess the situation? All her papers were in there, her clothes, what furniture she had, including the new bed and dresser in her bedroom. Surely everything was just wet and could be saved.

Forty minutes later Noelle had been assigned a cot in a segregated female section of the high school gymnasium. The men were on the opposite side of the cavernous space. The elderly woman who lived on her floor sat on her cot near Noelle, staring at nothing.

"Are you all right?" Noelle asked, sitting beside her and hugging her a moment.

"I can't believe we lost our home. We've lived in that apartment for thirty-three years. All we have is there," she said sadly.

"I don't think fire damaged our floor. If it's only water damage, we'll save most of our things," Noelle said, hoping it was true. She'd never felt so helpless—except the day Trevor had told her he was dying. She wanted to change everything, make the fire never happen, make Trevor never get sick. But life didn't work that way.

"Is Edward all right?" the elderly woman asked looking around.

"Your husband?" Noelle asked. At her nod, she looked over her shoulder. "All the guys are over on the other side. I see him near the edge. I'm sure you can go over and tell him good night."

"I can't imagine sleeping tonight. What are we going to do?"

Noelle wasn't sure about the next steps to be taken, but she was already wondering if more could have been done to alert the tenants sooner.

What has caused the fire? Why hadn't smoke alarms gone off or had they, but not on her floor? Maybe as part of their service, the owners should offer a check list of what do to for emergencies just like this. She didn't have duplicates of her important papers. Her valuable jewelry was merely sitting in a jewelry case on top of her dresser. Noelle didn't have a clue how to replace things like her marriage license or get another copy of Trevor's death certificate. There was so much the owners could address to offer more to their clients.

Or maybe Simpson and Mathias could come up with a checklist in case things went wrong. It could be part of their service to customers. She'd have to talk to Linc about the idea.

When the lights were dimmed in the huge gym, it was a clear signal it was time to sleep. While darker than it had been, Noelle could still see well enough to get to the doors. Several officials were at the hastily set up staging tables, talking quietly.

"Any word on when we might be able to return to our homes?" she asked.

"Not yet. The fire department hasn't finished. The fire is out, now they are trying to determine the cause. Once they do, and assess the damage and future safety of the building, we will have more information," one of the men said.

She thanked him and walked away a few steps. Taking her cell phone from her purse, she dialed Linc.

The phone rang several times. No wonder, it was four in the morning. Linc was still asleep.

"Mathias," he responded.

"Sorry to bother you at this time of night," Noelle said.

"What's wrong?" His voice sounded crisp and alert, not as if she'd just woken him.

"There was a fire—"

"At your place? Are you all right?"

"In my building and yes, I'm fine. But homeless for a while."

"Where are you now?"

"Some high school that's set up for emergencies. All of us from the apartment building are here. Almost half the building burned. I don't think my apartment was touched, except by water."

"Which high school? I'll come get you."

"I'll be fine here," she said.

But she wanted him to come for her. She wanted to be someplace she felt safe. She shivered again, still struggling with the reality of possibly losing her home and maybe some of her possessions.

"Which high school?" he repeated in a tone of voice that warned her not to argue any further.

She asked one of the officials and then told Linc. He said he'd be there in less than half an hour.

Noelle stayed with the people in the hall, not wanting to return to the gym where it was dark and quiet. The despair from everyone was almost tangible. When she heard the firm steps in the hallway, she looked and saw Linc striding toward her. Acting instinctively, she ran until she was enclosed in his strong arms and held tightly. For the first time since she'd woken she felt safe.

7

"Are you all right?" Linc asked again, holding her against him.

Noelle nodded, rubbing her cheek against his chest, reluctant to move an inch.

"Tired, and a bit cranky, but physically fine. We don't know the extent of the damage or when we can reenter the building. At least I had clothes on because I fell asleep reading. Most of the people here are in pajamas and robes. One woman was barefoot. Imagine how cold her feet must be standing on the bare concrete sidewalk. We watched and watched, until the fire was out. It was awful."

"Was anyone hurt?"

"Not that I know of."

"Be thankful for that. Come on, you're coming home with me."

She nodded and waved goodbye to the people at the table.

"I don't have any clothes to wear to work tomorrow. And I don't know if water damage has ruined everything I own."

"We'll see to all that when daylight arrives. For now, it's home and into bed with you."

Noelle was soon in the guest bed she'd used when she first arrived in San Francisco. She snuggled down in the covers, feeling chilled to the bone. Remembering Linc was only a few feet away had her warming up fast. She felt safe and secure and slowly she drifted to sleep.

When she awoke, it was mid morning. She raced from her room, but the rest of the apartment was empty. In the kitchen, propped up by the coffee maker, was a note from Linc.

Thought you needed your sleep. Call me when you wake up and I'll take you shopping. I'll check with the fire department on the status of your place."

She studied the bold handwriting, familiar from all the notes she'd seen over the years. No ending.

She tossed it down and poured herself a cup of hot coffee. What had she expected, love and kisses?

Not expected, but wouldn't have minded, she thought.

Here she was, full circle. She'd stayed at Linc's when she first came, waiting for her furniture and things. Now she could be stuck here a couple of days, waiting to see when she could return to her apartment.

She sipped her coffee and made plans. She could get a cab to Union Square and shop in some of the stores there. She needed the basics for a couple of days. Surely by then she could get back into her apartment. Today was Friday. She'd get two outfits, some undergarments and sleep wear. One new pair of shoes would tide her over. If for some reason she couldn't get back into her apartment soon, she'd go shopping for more things tomorrow afternoon.

No need to trouble Linc. He was not her keeper, much as Trevor had wanted.

At one-fifteen Noelle arrived at work. Harvey was the first to spot her and he came over to see how she was. Betty and two of the other women's operatives joined him in pelting her with questions.

Linc heard the noise and came out of his office and stared at her.

"I thought you were going to call me," he said.

"No need both of us being away from the office. I stopped at the store and got some things and here I am, ready to get back to work. Did you hear anything about when I can return to my apartment?"

She still carried the bags containing her old sweats and the new clothes she'd bought.

"Come with me. I'm sure everyone has things to do," Linc said, glancing around at the group.

The staff took the hint and fled.

Noelle wondered if she'd ever master that technique.

She followed Linc and put her shopping bags on one of the chairs.

"Sound like that isn't good news," she said.

He looked so much better today than yesterday. A night's sleep—even if interrupted—seemed to have done him a world of good. She knew she looked ragged. It wasn't fair.

"According to the fire marshal, they're still trying to verify the cause of the fire, but it points to wiring that wasn't up to code. If that's the case, the entire building will have to be rewired to code before they'll let the rest of the repairs commence."

"Which means no moving back in anytime soon."

"They also have to assess the structural damage, to see if it's safe for anyone to enter. They're hoping to let residents in one at a time over the weekend, to get what they need for the foreseeable future. However, no one will be moving back in soon."

"I liked that place," she said, sitting on one of the visitor chairs. "Now I have to start looking again. And who knows when I'll get my furniture out of there."

"I'll take you Saturday to get what we can carry out. Furniture will have to remain behind for the moment. But you can get your clothes and things."

"The jewelry Trevor gave me. Wouldn't Paul love knowing it's sitting unprotected in an empty building."

"With all the fire department personnel crawling over it, it's hardly unprotected. The cops will have it under surveillance until people get their valuables out. Don't worry about looting."

"No, I'll just worry about where I'm supposed to live."

"You'll stay with me until we know more. No need to make other plans," he said casually.

Noelle looked at him, her heart speeding up again. "Stay with you," she repeated slowly.

He shrugged. "Why not, you did when you first came. It's not likely to be that long."

She didn't say anything, but a million doubts flooded. To rewire an entire apartment building could take months. Then reconstruction of the damaged portion could take another set of months, always supposing the building was still structurally sound and could be repaired and not torn down.

Stay with Linc for weeks on end? She grew lightheaded just thinking about it.

"We'll see what the estimated time is," she finally said.

"Fair enough. You feel up to working today?"

"I wasn't hurt, just had my sleep interrupted. I'm fine."

Noelle made it through the rest of the day on autopilot, her thoughts focused on the coming evening. She'd stayed at Linc's apartment before–before the kiss, that was.

It had been weeks since then. If he had any interest in her, he would have shown it in the meantime. She had nothing to worry about—except her own reactions. Could she maintain a cool distance?

"Ready to leave?" Linc appeared in the doorway shortly after five.

"I'm ready."

"We need to stop at a supermarket. I wasn't expecting company."

"Fine."

It sounded so domestic. Somehow she never envisioned Linc shopping. It seemed too tame for him. Dining in expensive restaurants, grabbing a hot dog from a street vendor, she had no difficulty picturing him doing that. But mundane tasks like grocery shopping or stopping at the cleaners seemed for others, not someone like Linc Mathias.

A new side to the man, she thought with private amusement as they joined the other officer workers in the elevators.

He drove to the huge supermarket near the Marina. It carried everything from ten different varieties of all the staples to exotic Asian foods and Mexican selections.

It was also crowded.

Noelle was surprised to see so many young professionals pushing carts, talking. Flirting? She paid stricter attention. She looked at Linc to find his gaze was on her.

"What did you want to get?" she asked, feeling flustered by the look in those dark eyes.

"Enough food for a week or so."

"Surely I won't have to stay a week?"

"Who knows? In any event, I have to eat."

"What do you like?"

"What can you cook?"

Noelle gave him a slow smile. "Just about anything. You want some real home cooking? I'm happy to do it as payment for staying."

"I don't need any payment, Noelle. But I wouldn't say no to some good home cooking. I remember a couple of meals I had with you and Trevor."

"Okay, then, let me think a minute."

She quickly planned several dishes in her mind, and then looked around. "I don't know where everything is."

"We'll go up one aisle and down the other. But let's not take all night."

Forty minutes later they were back in the car, heading for Linc's apartment.

Noelle helped Linc put away the groceries then went to change before she began dinner. It was fun to be cooking for someone else again. Her solitary meals had been uninspired. There was nothing to get worked up about when cooking for one.

The lamb chops were grilling as she prepared a salad and popped the vegetables in the steamer. They'd have ice cream for dessert, but on Saturday, she'd bake a pie or cake. What did Linc like? She'd known Trevor's tastes, of course. But she hadn't a clue about her new partner's. He hadn't objected to any of the foods she'd bought so he probably liked everything.

"Need any help?" Linc asked, coming to stand too close for comfort.

Noelle drew in a deep breath and eased to the left a little. "I have everything under control. We'll be ready to eat in a moment."

He didn't move, just stood where he was, watching her.

She needed some space.

"Want to set the table?" she asked desperately.

He shrugged and stepped away. Noelle felt a shiver of anticipation. She had to get better control of her emotions if she planned to last until she could find somewhere else to live if her apartment wasn't ready soon.

When the meal was ready, she dished up the plates at the stove and handed one to Linc. Following him into the dining area, she was surprised to see he'd put their places next to one another. Swallowing hard, she put her plate down on one of the mats. He held her chair and she sat, wishing she'd set the table and put him at the head and her at the foot. But it was too late now. He sat beside her, his shoulder brushing against hers as he pulled his chair closer.

"Looks great," he said.

"I hope it tastes great," she murmured, conscious of the warmth from Linc's arm heating the scant space between them. She focused on the dinner, trying to ignore the way her body was growing more and more attuned to the man. For heaven's sake, she needed to eat and then get some rest. She hoped she could sleep through the night with no nightmares about the fire.

Actually she was hoping she could sleep period. She suspected her dreams would *not* be about the fire.

"I'll take you over to the apartment in the morning if that suits you," Linc said. "I usually take a run in the Park on Saturdays, so will be back around nine. As soon as I shower, we'll take off."

"That's fine." How could she think about tomorrow when she couldn't even think about dinner? She wanted to give into the urges that plagued her. Touch him, feel that warmth beneath her fingertips.

Did he think about their kiss? She reached for her water and took a long drink, hoping its coolness would help.

"Not hungry?" he asked. He had made inroads into the meat and vegetables but Noelle had scarcely touched her food.

"Yes." She took a big bite and chewed furiously. Tomorrow night, she'd set the table and make sure at least five feet separated them!

"Tell me about your trip," she said, taking another sip of water, and glancing at him as casually as she could. If she could get him talking, she'd have something to focus on beside his lips.

Only, when he began to speak, she couldn't look away. She watched his expressions, listened to his voice and let herself be swept away.

Noelle didn't remember eating, but most of her food was gone by the time Linc stopped talking. She jumped up and cleared their places.

He followed her into the kitchen, instantly making the room too small.

"Want ice cream?" he asked, opening the freezer.

"No, thanks. I'm really tired. I want to go to bed."

"Leave the dishes, then. I'll do them," he said.

She debated arguing, but needed the respite of her room.

"Thanks. I'll do them next time."

She smiled in his direction and hurried from the room. Only to be stopped by his hand on her arm. Gently he pulled her around.

"What's going on, Noelle?" he asked softly, his eyes boring down into hers.

"What do you mean?" She licked her lips.

"You're scurrying away like there's something wrong, that's all. You don't look that tired."

"I was up most of last night if you remember," she said.

"I do remember. I was up part of the night, too. This is your favorite ice cream, you said so at the store. Yet you don't want even a small helping?"

Her heart was beating heavily. Her skin tingled from his touch. Her gaze was captured by his. Her mind went blank. All she could do was feel the excitement being near him brought. Wanting and desire mixed with caution. This man could break her heart without half trying. She dared not go there.

"I'm tired," she said again.

"Then good night. I hope you sleep well."

She smiled. Before she could take a step toward the bedroom, however, he kissed her.

Noelle closed her eyes in astonishment, then responded. He released her arm to draw her into his embrace and she encircled his neck. Her mouth fused with his, her lips moving hungrily against his. The shock of desire pounded into her, making her wish for things that couldn't be. She wanted more. To be closer, to open herself up to this man, to learn his secrets and share hers.

His body was warm and hard against her softer one. His lips moved expertly against hers deepening the kiss.

Noelle had never felt the intensity of sensations that surged through her. He was all she could think about, all she could feel. She never wanted anything more from life but to be held by Linc, kissed by him, enthralled by him.

He brought the kiss to an end, moving to nibble along her cheek, bury his face against her neck, kissing where her shoulder and neck met. Her heart raced like the wind. She threaded her fingers through his thick hair, reveling in the feeling. Reckless in her behavior, she moved against him, pressing even closer, her mouth searching for his.

"Let me take care of this," he said, pushing against her shirt.

The words echoed in her mind. *Take care of. Take care of.* Trevor had made Linc swear to take care of her.

Reality slammed in with a vengeance. Noelle pushed against him, shrugging herself out of his arms.

"I don't *need* taking care of. I can manage my life myself," she said, turning and running down the hall. Had it only been a pity kiss? A prelude to some misbegotten feelings he owed Trevor?

She closed her door and leaned against it. Please don't let Trevor have voiced that crazy notion about getting married to Linc, she prayed.

"Noelle?" He knocked on the door.

"Go away," she said.

He ignored her and pushed open the door, shoving her halfway into the room. He stood there, glaring at her, still breathing hard from their kiss.

"What the heck is the matter with you?"

"I don't need taking care of."

"No one ever said you did," he replied.

"You just said you'd take care of me."

He groaned softly, rubbed his face with one hand. Slowly he dropped his hand and looked at her.

"What I said was let me take care of *this*—meaning removing your shirt."

"Why?"

He looked at her as if she were crazy. "Why does a man usually want to remove a woman's shirt—to get closer, of course. What do you think that was about in there?"

She didn't want to examine it too closely. She wanted to close the door and hide in the bed, until her apartment was ready and she could leave.

Only Trevor's words were still sounding in her head so she'd get no peace.

"A good-night kiss."

It sounded so lame. Especially after the erotic thoughts that had blossomed in her head. But she wouldn't tell him that. If he thought he owed Trevor, he'd do whatever necessary to pay him back.

But he didn't owe Trevor anything. And any promise made had to be taken with a grain of salt.

He crossed his arms across his chest.

"That was a pretty powerful good-night kiss. Are you all relaxed and ready for bed?"

Relaxed was the last thing she felt. And the only bed she was ready for was one she could share with Linc.

She turned and closed her eyes. Get a grip she admonished herself.

"I told you I was tired."

"My apologies."

A second later she heard the door close softly. Daring to peek behind her, she saw she was alone in the room.

Except for the memories permanently burned into her mind.

"Blast it all!" Linc said as he crossed the living room to the window and gazed out. He'd blown it completely. He'd be lucky if she stayed the night. Maybe tomorrow they'd find out her apartment would be ready soon. But if not, he had no expectations she'd stay in his until hers was ready. She'd be gone so fast it'd make his head spin.

He clenched his fists, wanting to lash out at something to ease his frustration. But there was only himself to blame.

He heard no sounds from Noelle's room. Was she still standing where he'd left her, or had she gone to bed?

Sighing softly, he turned and headed for the kitchen. Cleaning the dishes would give him something to do. Maybe he'd go for a run tonight as well. He was too keyed-up to sleep.

In the end, however, he settled for listening to some music and catching up on more reading. There were always reports and project updates to go through. Correspondence—some handled with an informational copy to him, some needing attention soon. He hoped Pam would soon come up to speed. He missed Betty's efficiency.

By the time he went to bed at eleven, he hadn't heard a single sound from Noelle. At least she hadn't left, he thought as he walked down the hall. Pausing outside her door, he hesitated. Slowly he reached out and turned the knob, easing the door open slightly. She was in bed, fast asleep. He studied her for a long moment, then closed the door. He had some fences to mend. He didn't want her moving out.

Noelle awoke refreshed. Despite her fears, she'd slept dreamlessly and deeply. Taking a quick shower, she dressed in her new jeans and top. It was almost ten. She'd slept as late as yesterday. While someone could get used to that, she normally woke much earlier. She wanted to get back on her own schedule, in her own place.

Taking a fortifying breath, she ventured out of her room into the apartment. It was silent. The aroma of coffee filled the air.

She walked into the kitchen. As when she'd stayed before, Linc had started the coffee brewing. She poured a cup. He was on his run, she knew. How long before he returned and she had to face him? Quickly she prepared herself some oatmeal and ate it. She didn't really need his help in finding out about her apartment. She could walk over. It looked as if it was a nice day.

She heard the front door. Another fortifying breath, just in time. He walked into the kitchen, looking like every woman's fantasy. His long, muscular legs were tanned beneath the running shorts. The T-shirt he wore molded his chest and shoulders like a second skin, highlighting the breadth and sculptured muscles. His hair was wind tossed and her fingers itched with remembered longing. Had she run them through that thick hair only last night? It seemed like an eternity ago. And only seconds past.

"Good morning," he said, as if nothing had ever happened between them.

"Good morning," she replied, watching him warily.

He got a glass and filled it with water, drinking the entire glassful in only a moment.

"I'll be ready as soon as I shower," he said, leaving without looking at her.

Feeling deflated, Noelle nodded. Not that he saw. He was already gone.

"We're two adults, who shared a hot kiss. I can handle that," she told herself, rinsing her bowl.

She took her coffee and went to the living room, standing near the window. She missed her veranda in Virginia. She and Trevor had loved having coffee outside on nice days.

The intense pain at missing Trevor didn't surface. She waited, but only a feeling of sad nostalgia rose. Was she already getting over his death?

Panic flared. She didn't want to. She wanted to mourn him forever. He'd been such a wonderful man—loving and caring.

What kind of woman stopped grieving her husband because another man kissed her?

She was still by the window, trying to make sense of things, when Linc joined her.

"Ready?" He stood near the door.

Noelle turned and nodded. She set her cup down on the table and went to get her purse. Linc seemed different this morning, more remote. Was he having regrets over last night, too?

Perversely she didn't want that. He was entitled to kiss whomever he wanted. And for one glorious moment, he'd wanted to kiss her.

The drive to the apartment was short. Parking was impossible when they reached the building. There were construction vehicles, city cars and the regular automobiles of residents of the other apartment buildings on the block.

"Drop me and I'll find out what I can," Noelle suggested.

"I'll find a place. You don't want to go alone."

"Yes, I do."

She needed to show Linc, as if in some convoluted way she could prove to Trevor, that she could manage on her own. She didn't need taking care of.

He slowed as he searched for a spot and she opened the door. He slammed on the brakes.

"Are you crazy?"

She slipped from the car and leaned back in.

"No, just determined. Circle around. When I'm done, I'll catch you."

Shutting the door, she nimbly made her way to the sidewalk. She hadn't a clue which person to ask so continued walking toward the lobby. Surely there'd be someone somewhere who knew the status.

The smell of smoke was heavy in the air. The building looked worse this morning, with the charred timbers thrusting up against the clear blue sky. She looked at the windows of her own apartment. They had been broken, as most of the ones on that side of the building had been. The heat of the fire or the actions of the firefighters? She wasn't sure.

"Can I help you, miss?" a burly man with a clipboard stopped her near the front door, just as Noelle recognized Thelma and Edward, her across the hall neighbors. She smiled at them, then turned to the man.

"I'm Noelle Simpson, Apartment 4 C. When can I get back inside?"

He consulted his clipboard. Glanced up at the apartment. "We're staggering people going in to minimize the impact on the building. Fourth Floor is scheduled for eleven-thirty. You'll have half an hour to get what you want, then you have to evacuate so the next floor has their turn."

"We have to get our things? What about moving back in?"

"Lady, it'll be months before this place is habitable again, if then. They may just raze it to the ground and start over."

"I can't possibly get all my things out of there in thirty minutes. I have furniture, clothes, books."

The task would be overwhelming. Even if she could schedule a moving company to get there by eleven-thirty, there'd be no way they could clear her apartment in thirty minutes.

"Sorry, lady. That's the way it's going to be today. Take what you can carry and what you need for the next few weeks. There will be other days when they'll be open for furniture removal."

He handed her a sheet of paper with phone numbers, contact names, moving companies and other information.

"Call that number on Monday, to get an appointment to get the rest of your things out. They won't start renovations until everyone has vacated their space."

"Hello, dear," Thelma said, coming up to Noelle. "Isn't it terrible? Edward and I don't know what we're going to do. We've been moved to a small motel near downtown. But we can't afford to stay there until the apartment is renovated. Where did you get to?"

"I had a friend come get me. I'm staying with him temporarily. Otherwise, I guess I'd be homeless. I can't believe they may raze the place. How bad was the fire?"

"Pretty bad," Edward said, following behind his wife. "I think I heard the fire exposed all the code violations which have to be met now before they'll issue certificates of occupancy again. With rent control, this place was perfect for us. We could so easily afford it. Now, we'll be hunting at today's rates. With a fixed retirement income, I don't think we'll find anything in the city we can afford."

"I'm sure you'll find something else," Noelle said, hoping it was true.

Though she knew herself how expensive housing was in San Francisco. Hadn't it taken her several days of hunting to find something she liked and could afford and that was with the help of Betty.

"I'm not so sure," Thelma said sadly.

Linc joined her. Noelle looked at him in surprise. "Found a parking place?"

"Couple of blocks over. What's going on?"

She told him, then introduced her neighbors. The four of them moved to the edge of the sidewalk, deciding to wait together until their allotted time to go in.

When Noelle walked up the fire stairs to the fourth floor, the smoke smell was stronger than ever. The hallway seemed forlorn, the wet carpet squished underfoot. The bright red sticker on her door reminded her of the fireman's hurried questions to make sure the apartment was empty when she left.

She opened the door. Cold damp air met her. Two windows were broken, the wet carpet contained puddles of standing water.

"It's a mess," Linc said unnecessarily.

Sadly she looked at her furniture, her sodden magazines, the wet afghan on the back of her sofa. "It could have been worse," she said. "At least I do still have my furniture."

"Let's go, we're down to twenty-seven minutes," Linc said, heading for the small drop-front desk. "I'll pack up your desk."

"I have some plastic bags in the kitchen. Even if they got wet, we can use them to carry things," Noelle said, shaking off the feeling of depression and crossing to her small kitchen unit. With no window, it hadn't been subject to as much water as the other parts of the apartment. She pulled out all the bags she had and went back, giving a handful to Linc.

"I'll start with my clothes," she said, continuing to the bedroom.

Thirty minutes went quickly. One of the security guards for the apartment knocked on the door. "Time's up, ma'am," he said when Noelle went there. Linc had already made several trips carrying bags to his car. There were half a dozen sitting by the front door, all she had been able to pack.

"We're ready."

She had most of her important things: jewelry, clothes, papers. The furniture she couldn't take, but knew she could arrange a moving company to come at an allotted time in the near future. At least with the windows broken, the air would circulate and hopefully dry things out before they were totally ruined.

"This feels so weird," she said ten minutes later when she and Linc headed for his apartment, his car jammed with her possessions.

"This time last year I was wondering what to do about Thanksgiving with Trevor's family. Now, I'm a widow with no place to live, far from home and friends."

Linc looked at her. "You're not going to cry, are you?"

"No, I'm not. If I did, what would you do?"

"Panic," he said.

She smiled. The man had never known a moment's panic in his life. "Life sure throws curves."

"You're not homeless, you're staying with me. You're not far from friends, you've made some here and your friends in Virginia are only a phone call away."

Noelle nodded. All true, but she felt homeless, and lonely.

They unpacked the car and Noelle spent most of the afternoon going through her things, washing her clothes to get rid of the smoky smell and the water stains. Some of her papers were wet, so she spread those out to dry.

Restless while waiting for another load of laundry to finish, she went to the kitchen and began to make a coconut cake. Baking was soothing and something she loved to do.

As she was frosting the cake some time later, she gave thought to what to have for dinner. Fried chicken came to mind. It was comfort food and today she needed some comfort. Plus, men loved fried chicken. She'd bought plenty of chicken when she and Linc had gone shopping. There was a casserole she liked with chicken, too. But tonight she opted for comfort food.

She had the pieces frying in the oil when she heard the front door. She hadn't seen Linc all afternoon. He'd said something about going to the office. Had he really been afraid she was going to cry earlier? She smiled again at the memory of his succinct answer.

The first of the fried chicken was draining on paper towels as the next batch browned in the hot oil. Her homemade biscuits were cut out and on the pan ready to pop into the oven. Vegetables were simmering on the stove. It was a little early to eat, but she was hungry, and after being at work all afternoon, she suspected Linc would be as well.

He appeared in the doorway.

Seeing what she was doing, he looked taken aback.

"Darn, I'm not going to be home for dinner," he said.

It took a minute for the words to sink in. She looked at all the chicken she'd cooked. Enough for tonight and tomorrow for lunch. Entirely too much for a single person.

"Oh?"

The biscuits were ready to cook and the cake sat in splendor on the counter.

"I should have told you. It slipped my mind with the fire and getting your things and all. I, uh, have already made dinner plans," he said.

A date.

She felt a sinking sensation.

Linc was going out on a date. And it wasn't with her.

What was she thinking? He had every right to go out with whomever he wished. She had plenty to do–she could finish her laundry and check to see if her papers had dried out.

Tears threatened. She'd planned such a nice dinner–but he'd rather go out with someone else.

"That's okay. The good thing about fried chicken is that it tastes as good cold the next day."

She dared not look at him. He was too astute to not notice how the news had hit her.

"I'm sorry."

"No, don't be. Really, it's okay. Go and have fun."

She held her breath, willing him to leave before she made a fool of herself.

He stayed in the doorway for another moment, then left. She heard him close the door to his room.

Getting dressed to take somebody out to dinner.

Why did it hurt so much? Linc was her partner, they ran a business together. Actually he did more of the running, but she felt she was making a definite contribution with the new women's safety project.

If she'd been at her apartment tonight, she'd never have known that he was going out.

Unless she'd invited him to dinner and been turned down.

She was so pathetic mooning over a man who thought of her as his best friend's wife.

She finished the batch of chicken and put the remaining pieces in. Her appetite had fled, but she'd finish preparing the meal and eat it. Maybe she'd go out to the local bookstore after dinner and find an excellent book that would capture her imagination and keep her occupied through the evening.

"I won't be late," Linc said a few minutes later.

She looked at the doorway, wishing she hadn't. He looked gorgeous. His dark suit and pristine white shirt set off his tanned skin. The dark red tie gave the finishing touches, not that he needed any embellishments. He'd cause heads to turn wherever he went—especially from the women.

Her emotions under tight control, Noelle smiled and waved.

"Have fun," she said. "Don't hurry home on my account. I have plans for after dinner."

"What plans?" he asked sharply.

She was taken aback by his question, and attitude. "What do you care?" she asked, stalling for something better to say than going to a bookstore.

He drew in a deep breath. "Curiosity."

"Don't worry about me, I'll be fine. You go on now, you don't want to be late."

He hesitated a second, as if he had something further to say, then turned and left.

Noelle was puzzled by his reaction.

Later, at the bookstore, Noelle got a stack of books and went to the coffee bar section. Settling at one of the tables with a tall coffee, she perused each one, trying to see if the subject matter had any appeal. Sipping the hot beverage, she glanced around. There were couples with their heads close together, talking softly. Two guys at separate tables busy with laptops. Another single woman was leafing through a magazine, an empty dessert plate and coffee cup to one side. Noelle felt a moment of kinship with her.

She chose two books, knowing she had to put the others back, but not making a move. The coffee bar was bustling and she loved to people watch. It beat returning to an empty apartment whose owner was out on the town, probably with some fabulously beautiful blonde. She couldn't see Linc going out with anyone who wasn't accomplished and entertaining. He was too dynamic to put up with a shy woman.

Would he like someone who deferred to his every wish? Or did he prefer the spark of an opposing opinion–not getting his way in everything?

She realized she didn't know him as much as she thought she did. He'd avoided her over the last few years, ever since he'd moved to the West Coast.

She'd missed him more than she'd thought she would.

She looked at her hand. Slowly she withdrew her wedding ring. She was no longer married. Hard as it was to admit, she was now single.

And unless she wanted to remain alone on all the Saturday nights in the future, she had to start seeing other people again. Other men. She'd liked being married and she couldn't envision the rest of her life living alone.

Maybe she wasn't quite ready to marry just yet. But she was ready to start living again. Trevor had told her over and over those last weeks to move on, to celebrate life, do everything she could that he no longer could do. Make love, have children–and name one for him.

Tears blurred her vision. She blinked, hoping no one saw. Gathering her books, she went to replace the ones she didn't want. It was time to honor her promises to Trevor and really move on.

8

Noelle rose early on Sunday. Once dressed, she went to the kitchen to fix a picnic lunch with the leftovers from last night's dinner. She packed chicken, biscuits, some celery and a large piece of coconut cake. A bottle of cold water from the refrigerator completed her meal. She had it all in her backpack and was ready to walk out the door when she heard Linc.

Darn, she'd wanted to be gone by the time he got up. She hadn't heard when he'd come in last night, but it was after she went to bed, so it wasn't as early a night as he'd suggested.

"What are you doing?" he asked. Dressed for running, he hadn't yet shaved.

She swallowed at the intimate morning scene. Her heart kicked into high gear again. She was getting tired of her reaction around the man. She longed for peace and tranquility, and instead she got hot and bothered.

"I'm going to Golden Gate Park for the day. There are some wonderful walking trails, and I want to see the Conservatory of Flowers. I heard it's a must-see."

"I was going running, but if you wait a few minutes until I get dressed, I'll go with you," he said.

"No need. I wanted to explore on my own."

She did not want this man with her all day long. She wasn't sure she could maintain any distance if he spent that much time with her.

"You don't want me along?" he asked.

She shook her head.

"Why not? Trevor said to watch out for you."

"That's why. I'm all grown up and I can manage perfectly well on my own. I want to see something of San Francisco besides the financial district."

"What if I said I wanted to take you, not for Trevor, but for me," he asked.

She paused a heartbeat. "I don't think that would be a good idea."

"I think it's a great idea. Add enough food for me." He turned, then stopped, looking over his shoulder. "Did you have breakfast?"

She shook her head, still debating whether to add food or flee the minute he reached his bedroom.

"We'll go to Sharlies. It's got the best bagels in town."

Linc went to his room and changed into jeans and a pullover. Getting a jacket—October was nice, but not that warm—he debated shaving. But from the skittish way Noelle was acting, he didn't dare delay.

Last night had been a monumental mistake. He'd seen the meal she'd prepared, and the disappointment in her eyes when he'd told her he was going out. He'd felt an inch tall.

She didn't want him to go with her today, but he wasn't about to let the opportunity pass. It was time she got out and started living again. Trevor wanted the best for her. The man had been crazy about her, despite the age difference.

Linc wondered when Trevor first told him he was seeing her if it was an attempt to recapture his youth. But the man had genuinely fallen for Noelle. Who wouldn't? Linc thought. She'd made Trevor very happy.

Had she been as happy as Trevor? Not since his death.

Linc wanted to chase away the sadness from her eyes. Show her there were lots of ways to live. She needed to grab for the gusto, as the old slogan went, and he'd be happy to show her how.

When he returned to the kitchen, Noelle was just closing her backpack. He hoped that meant she'd added enough food for him.

"Aren't you going for your run?" she asked. "We could meet up some place later."

"I can skip a day or two. Have you had Sharlies bagels?"

She shook her head.

"They are hot from the oven. Slather a flavored cream cheese on them and it's the best breakfast in the city. Got all you need?"

She nodded and lifted the backpack.

Linc reached over and took it. "I'll carry this."

It wasn't that heavy, but there was no need for her to carry it. Besides, they wouldn't get separated if he had her lunch.

They drove the short distance to the bagel shop and Linc found a parking place only a block away. As they walked back, Noelle commented, "We could have walked this distance."

"True. But then we'd have to walk back to get the car. It's too far to walk to Golden Gate Park and then hike around the park and walk home. Though if you want to train for a marathon, it'd be a good run."

The bagel store was crowded. The line serpentined as people patiently waited their turn to order. In the back, huge vats of boiling water gave off clouds of steam. The oven's shelves were constantly rotating and spilling out hot bagels. The glass-front counter displayed all the varieties the shop offered. Seven people waited on the customers, and still the line was long.

Noelle glanced at the crowded tables. "Think we'll find a place?" she asked, stepping a bit closer to Linc to let a man pass.

Linc threw his arm around her shoulder and gently urged her to move in front of him, out of the line of traffic. He felt the tension rise but didn't remove his arm.

"If not, we'll walk back to the car and eat them as we go. But I think the turnover is pretty fast, so we should get something."

He could smell Noelle's own special fragrance over the aromas of the cooking bagels.

She always smelled fresh and sweet. Was it her soap or did she wear some perfume?

She continued to stand stiffly. He wanted her to relax—preferably against him.

When the line moved, he shifted positions and put both hands on her shoulders, loathe to break the contact. Leaning forward slightly, he spoke softly in her ear.

"What kind are you going to have? I can recommend the poppy seed ones, onion ones and the cheddar cheese."

She looked over her shoulder and Linc felt a stab of desire. Her face was only inches from his. It would take so little to lean a bit closer and kiss her. For a moment he envisioned doing that. But it was neither the time nor the place. Much as he wanted to kiss Noelle, he'd bide his time. He was not looking for a kiss-and-run date. He wanted more from her. With her.

"Which are you having today?" she asked.

From the way her gaze focused on his mouth, Linc knew he wasn't the only one thinking about a kiss.

"I'm having the poppy seed with one of the flavored cream cheeses."

"I might try that as well," she said, turning her head back to face forward.

By the time they picked up their order, there were several tables available. Taking one near the front windows, Linc sat opposite Noelle. The coffee smelled delicious. The warm bagels were chewy and fresh. He watched Noelle daintily try the one she'd gotten, enjoying the look of supreme satisfaction on her face.

"Delicious!" she said. "Good choice. You come here often?"

"Most weekends. I usually go for a run and stop by to pick them up and take them back to the apartment to eat. These are better—still warm."

He looked at her hand as she raised the bagel for another bite. Her ring was missing.

"What happened to your wedding ring?" he asked.

"I took it off when I was out last night. I'm not married anymore."

For a moment, he wondered what had prompted that. "Where did you go?"

"To that bookstore near the wharf."

He wanted to ask if she'd met someone there, but didn't know how to do so without sounding like an idiot. She was entitled to meet whomever she wished, wherever she wished.

Linc ate his own bagel, wondering how much damage he'd done to their relationship by going out last night. He hadn't even enjoyed the evening. It was nothing against Salina, but he'd wanted to be with Noelle. Because he felt guilty at the thought, he'd done his best to make sure Salina had a great evening, staying out far longer than he'd wanted. It wasn't her fault his attention was elsewhere.

Noelle had been in bed by the time he got home. He'd noticed the light was off when he'd passed her door on the way to his room.

What had made her take off her ring?

He wasn't one to look back. The evening had gone as it had gone. He wasn't going to regret the lost opportunity to spend time with her. He hadn't known when he invited Salina out that Noelle would again be living with him. Or apparently ready to move on. Was that an indication to him?

Noelle was living with him. It sounded more intimate than it was.

Maybe he should change that. Show her that living with him was good. If he could talk her into staying while they repaired her apartment building, he'd have an open line directly to her social life. She had to be ready to test the waters. He was certainly ready.

"Are you all right?" Noelle asked.

He looked at her, bringing her face into focus. "Of course, why?"

"You haven't eaten in five minutes and you have a faraway look on your face."

"Just thinking about things," he said, taking a bite.

She'd already finished her bagel and was sipping the last of her coffee.

"Like what?"

He looked at her. "Like, do you ever think about getting married again?"

The look of horror on her face was almost amusing. What was wrong with the question? he wondered. It was perfectly logical in light of her removing her ring.

"Trevor didn't tell you to marry me, did he?" she asked.

It was Linc's turn to be surprised. "No, of course not!"

He studied her expression; it was a mixture of relief and wariness. What on earth was going on? Then it clicked.

"He told you to *marry* me?" he exclaimed. *Trevor, you idiot!*

She took a sip of coffee, and carefully replaced the cup on the table. She looked at him, then away, then back again.

"He was worried about me going on after he died. I told him I'd be fine, but he insisted you needed to be involved."

Linc nodded once, remembering having a similar conversation with Trevor.

She took a deep breath. "Once he said that it would solve everything if I married you."

She tried to smile, but it didn't reach her eyes. "He was joking, of course."

"Was he?" Linc pressed.

"Yes. I'm not going to marry someone because it solves problems. I'm perfectly capable of taking care of myself. I don't need to marry to do that. If I marry again, and I don't know at this point that I will, it will be because I'm wildly in love, not as an expediency."

Good going, Trevor, Linc thought in frustration. Another roadblock. What were you thinking, my friend? Didn't you know your wife better than that?

"Then I guess I won't be proposing to you today," he joked, wadding his napkin into a ball and tossing it onto the table. "You ready to go?"

"You won't be proposing ever. I'm not getting married as a matter of convenience," she said firmly.

"If I haven't married by now, it's unlikely I'll do so at my age, don't you think?" he said, rising. This conversation wasn't going at all like he wanted. It was time to change the subject.

"We can see the Conservatory first, then I know a quiet glade that would be perfect for lunch," he said, heading for the door. The crowd hadn't diminished, and they wove their way through the people.

"I'm not hungry after that breakfast," Noelle said when they reached the sidewalk.

"That's why I thought the Conservatory first, then it's a bit of a walk from there to the spot I'm thinking of. We'll have time to work off breakfast."

And maybe give him some inkling of what he was going to do about Noelle Simpson.

Noelle loved the Conservatory. The flowers were exotic

and lovely, still blooming even late in October. There was a butterfly room and she was enchanted by the fluttering creatures. She'd come again, she knew.

The walk along the pathway that wound through part of Golden Gate Park was delightful. The air was full of the scent of eucalyptus. The tall trees shaded the walkway, making it cooler than expected. Linc set a brisk pace.

"If we go any faster, you'll have that run you missed earlier," she commented at one point, getting out of breath.

"Too fast?"

"Faster than I want, I can't really enjoy what I'm seeing. But it helps keep me warm."

"You should have worn more than a sweater," he said. "It's cooler here near the ocean than at the apartment."

"I'll know for next time," she murmured.

They passed others walking in the opposite direction, but there were few people on the path. Sometimes it opened up and she could see a meadow and the tops of building surrounding the large natural park. Other times she felt as if she were in an enclosed walkway, with only Linc—the two of them alone in a world of their own. It was hard to believe the hectic, frenetic pace of San Francisco was only a few hundred yards away. Here it was peaceful and quiet.

Trevor would have liked it, she thought.

"Did you stumble?" Linc asked.

He seemed acutely attuned to her every action.

"I was thinking Trevor would have liked this."

"Would he?"

Linc had never gone on nature walks with Trevor. They'd

played tennis and gone sailing a couple of times.

"What was it like being married to a man so much older than you?" he asked.

"I loved Trevor," she replied quickly. She knew at one time Linc had questioned that. "I didn't marry him for his money."

"I know. But he *was* so much older than you. A different generation, actually. It had to make some kind of change in your life. In the way you probably once thought about being married."

Noelle didn't know how to answer without sounding disloyal to Trevor.

"Things were a bit different, but it wasn't as if he were an invalid or anything. He was already established and had that huge family trust fund, so money worries weren't there. He had his house, I moved into it and brought little with me. I guess if I'd really thought about it, I would have liked us to have a house that was ours. I always felt it was his."

She bit her lip. There was more she could say, but she didn't want to tell Linc.

Trevor had loved her, had done his best to make her happy. When she'd voiced disagreeing opinions, he'd always had a logical reason for choosing his way over hers.

The house had only been one example. Why move and incur additional expenses when that house was already there, he was already living in it, and it was fully funded by the trust, Trevor had said.

It was logical. But sometimes, Noelle didn't want to live only by logic.

"I can see that would be a problem—most women like to have a home of their own," Linc said.

"It was fine. It was his family home and I was a part of his family, despite what Paul thinks."

"He still giving you trouble?"

"Not anymore than he's been doing since Trevor died. My attorney sent a formal notice to stop harassing me as he reviews the trust to see if there is any violation. I'm sure Trevor didn't do anything wrong."

"Paul's a man who needs to get a life."

Noelle laughed. "You're right. Oh, this is lovely."

They had reached a small walkway leading to an open grassy area, full of sunlight, surrounded by trees and shrubbery. It was deserted. They stepped off the path to the grass and wandered to the center of the clearing.

"I'm glad it's empty. Not many people know about it," Linc said.

He slung down the backpack. "Did you bring a blanket to sit on?"

She nodded. "It's under the food, I didn't want it crushing anything. Let me unpack."

Noelle knelt on the grass and opened the backpack, withdrawing the food she'd carefully packed. Then the throw she'd thought to use when she'd planned a solo outing. It wasn't as large for two as she could wish.

In only moments they were enjoying the cold fried chicken.

"While I'm sorry I missed your dinner last night, I'm glad there were leftovers," Linc said. "You're a good cook."

"Thanks. I like to cook for more than one. It's hardly worth it when it's only me."

"Did you cook for you and Trevor?"

"Of course. Most of the time, anyway. Whenever we entertained, he insisted on having the dinner catered. He wanted me available to mingle not be tied to the kitchen."

"Sounds nice."

She shrugged.

Once again, it had been a point Trevor had insisted upon. She would have liked to cook some of her special recipes for friends.

Looking around the glen, she smiled.

"This is so peaceful. It's hard to believe San Francisco is just beyond those trees."

"It's a good place to get away when things get stressful," Linc said. "I bet you'll love the Japanese Tea Garden, we'll go there after we eat."

"Or we can just stay here for a while," Noelle said, growing sleepy with the food and the warmth from the sun. She wouldn't mind taking a nap in the fresh air.

"If you like," Linc said.

Linc told her of the history of the Park and some other stories of San Francisco from the early days.

When she finished eating, she cleared a place and lay down.

"Going to sleep?" he asked.

"Keep talking, I like listening to you," she said. "Tell me more about the Barbary Coast."

Before long his voice seemed to grow faint and she drifted to sleep.

When Noelle awoke the sun was no longer overhead. Shadows were creeping across the glade. She turned her head and almost bumped into Linc. He was asleep.

Probably because of his late night, she thought, frowning and sitting up. It was so quiet she could hear birds rustling in the trees. She caught a glimpse of a couple strolling along the main path, then they were lost from view.

Turning, she studied Linc. She'd never seen him asleep before. His face didn't look much softer in repose than when he was awake.

He was taller than Trevor and in better physical shape. Of course, he was twenty years or more younger than Trevor had been.

She shifted a little, gazing into the past. What would have happened if Trevor had not asked her out? Would Linc ever have asked her?

She'd have gone out with him without hesitation. Even married happily for years hadn't completely erased the awareness she always felt around him. If she had to explain it, she'd call it chemistry.

Would it have led them anywhere? Or after a few dates, a few kisses, would the attraction have worn out?

She'd never know. Because how would she ever be sure any attention to her from Linc wasn't a result of Trevor's last request?

"Ready to go?" Linc asked.

She looked at him. His eyes were watching her. How long had he been awake?

"Sure, let's find that Tea Garden."

He sat up, much closer than comfortable. His shoulder brushed hers. Her eyes were locked with his. Slowly his head came near. Did hers move to close the distance?

When his lips covered hers, she gave up any pretense of resistance, moving to meet his kiss.

Noelle felt herself falling. Linc pulled her down with him on the blanket until they were lying side by side. His mouth moved against hers, his tongue teasing her lips until they opened for him. He deepened the kiss, his hands pulling her closer. She felt every inch of his hard body against hers.

Excitement made her heart race and her skin tingled every place he touched it. She wanted more, then was shocked to realize how alive she felt. Alive and young and carefree. She forgot about the past and the future. Only this moment mattered.

She gave into temptation and let her hands caress him, feeling the warmth of his skin through the cotton shirt he wore, the strength of his muscles playing against her palms.

Noelle could have kissed Linc forever, but a finger of shade blocked the warmth of the sun. The coolness surprised her and broke the spell.

She pushed him away and sat up, breathing hard. He was too dangerous to be around. She had absolutely no willpower to resist, and who knew what kind of trouble that could get her into? He was her partner, her late husband's partner. He could be nothing more.

"You okay?" he asked.

She nodded.

"Fine. I think we should go now."

She scrambled to her feet and repacked the remnants of lunch. She couldn't fold the blanket until Linc got off it. But she wasn't looking at him. She couldn't depend on her own good sense. What if one look at him and she threw herself into his arms and demanded he kiss her until it turned dark?

He rose easily and reached out to capture her chin, turning it up until she faced him.

"It was only a kiss, Noelle. You're single, I'm single. What's a kiss?"

"It's too soon."

"Because?"

"Trevor hasn't been dead a year yet."

"And a year is a magic number?"

"Don't people mourn for a year before moving on?"

"I don't think there is a set time. On one level, I think I'll mourn his passing until I die. On another, I've adjusted to his being gone from the business. Gotten used to not being able to call him on a question about the company or just to talk. He didn't want you to remain a widow all your life. You're young, Noelle, not even thirty. You can't mourn him forever."

"Maybe I can," she said, wishing it was easier to know what she wanted.

But with Linc's hand against her skin, she was having trouble thinking at all. She tried to hold on to Trevor's memory, but she couldn't see his face.

She could only stare at Linc, feel the sensations his touch caused. How could she be unfaithful to a man she'd loved for years?

"You can't mourn forever," he repeated and leaned in for another kiss.

Noelle closed her eyes and held on. His kiss was all she'd ever wanted in an embrace, exciting, erotic, and full of promise. Had she ever felt so strongly for Trevor? She couldn't remember.

She could hardly remember her own name with Linc's mouth moving against hers. Being with Linc brought her to a new height in awareness of her own femininity. She wanted to explore those new feelings, see what being with Linc would be like. Would he be an ardent lover? One whose skills would be all a woman could ever hope for? Or was it all an illusion?

Voices sounded from the path and Linc ended the kiss. He smiled slightly, brushing his thumb across her lips.

"You look beautiful," he said.

Noelle turned away and bent to retrieve the backpack. She wasn't sure if she was glad for the interruption or regretted it. But at least it gave her time to think and decide what the next step should be.

"Let's go to the Tea Gardens," she said, avoiding his eyes.

Her heart pounded as if she'd run a race. Her skin felt sensitized as the breeze floated over her. The colors surrounding her looked brighter, sharper.

Linc fell into step with her. "It's a bit of a walk."

"I planned to spend the day here. Lead on."

After those kisses, the last place Noelle wanted to be was back at the apartment—alone with Linc. She needed to fill the day with activities to grow tired enough to sleep without dreaming at night.

Tomorrow was Monday and she could get back to her normal work schedule.

There were more people in the park now or they were moving into a more popular area. Couples, families and the occasional jogger crowded the pathway. Several times they had to walk single-file to avoid running into someone.

When they reached the Japanese Tea Gardens, Noelle was delighted. Linc was right, the setting was spectacular. Traditional Japanese garden displays were showcased to perfection. Every where she looked, she felt the peace of the place. She knew she'd come back time and again.

She sat on a stone bench and looked at the various shades of green, the simple design of rock, plants and gravel. Linc sat beside her. He didn't say anything and she was touched by his sensitivity. Had he picked up on her need for serenity after that disturbing interlude in the glade?

Or was she the only one disturbed? To him she was probably just another woman. He'd gone out with someone last night. Had he kissed her the same way?

Noelle frowned, disliking the thought of Linc kissing anyone else.

"Don't like the view?" he asked lazily.

"It's spectacular."

"Why the frown."

Like she'd tell him her confused thoughts. "Just thinking of things."

"If you're thinking about the kisses, don't. You're a beautiful, single woman. I'm a single guy. There's no harm done."

Except to make Noelle wonder how being married to Linc would be compared to Trevor. She'd been happy in her marriage, but a few kisses from her late husband's partner and she wondered if she'd experienced all she should have in that union. Her husband had been older, not nearly as virile or passionate as Linc. She'd had no one to compare him to and so had enjoyed their life together.

But she couldn't remember a single day when she felt as stirred up with Trevor as she did with Linc.

What did that say about her marriage? About her?

"It's getting cool, ready to head back?" he asked a few moments later.

"Yes. I have some work to do before tomorrow," she said. That'd give her an excuse to remain in her room this evening and not be tempted.

Linc watched the expressions cross her face and almost kicked himself. He'd moved too fast again, but patience wasn't his strong suit. She'd thrown up barriers once more and seemed to grow more remote the longer they sat together.

He wouldn't forget her response to his kisses. She'd been like liquid fire in his arms. Had she felt anything like he had or was she just grateful for affection? He didn't buy into the fallacy that widows miss a man. Some might, some might not. But if they did, it was usually their husband they missed.

He knew Noelle missed Trevor. She mentioned him frequently. Not with great grief, but with sweet nostalgic memories. Maybe there was a timetable for grief, he didn't know. But Noelle had to wake up to the real world sometime and maybe he could nudge her along.

He wasn't sure where he wanted things to go. Staring at the artful arrangement of low-growing bushes and rock, he felt the uncertainty that being with her brought. He'd always wonder if things would have gone differently if he'd asked her out before Trevor. Maybe they'd have had a terrible time and she'd have been happy to go out with Trevor if he'd then asked her.

But Linc didn't really believe that for a moment. Every second he spent with Noelle was all he could ask for. She was intelligent, with a wide, eclectic interest in so many different things, she was never boring.

And she was ambitious and smart—look at how well the new women's safety plan was growing. She had the makings of a very successful businesswoman.

Exciting to be with, interesting to talk to, and sexy as anyone he'd ever known.

Which left him where? Nowhere as long as she thought any attention he paid her was due to some death-bed promise to Trevor.

He couldn't deny the promise. But there was more to his interest than taking care of his partner's widow.

Though how he was going to make her believe that was beyond him right now.

And how far did he want to go?

All the way to marriage?

He looked at Noelle.

She rose. "Okay, I'm ready to go," she said.

She still hadn't looked at him. Was she disgusted he'd kissed her? Did she want to forget it had ever happened?

He knew he never would.

Rising, Linc let her proceed him from the gardens.

Whatever it took, he wanted to keep the lines of communication open. And watch to see when she was ready. For now he wouldn't push, but he was not a patient man. He knew what he wanted and he'd go after it just like every other goal he'd set himself.

When they returned to the apartment, Noelle thanked him politely for the day and headed for her room, claiming work.

"I'll order Chinese in for dinner if you like," he called after her, annoyed she preferred work to his company.

She stuck her head out of her doorway and nodded. "Call me when it's here." She closed her door and Linc was left standing in the hall.

He'd been the perfect companion on the walk back to the car and the ride to the apartment, commenting on the aspects of the Park he thought she'd like. Then pointing out one or two landmarks of San Francisco. She had been as responsive as a tongue-tied teenager.

He shook his head. She frustrated him. He glanced at his watch. There were still a couple of hours until dinner time. Maybe he'd take that run he'd postponed from the morning, get rid of some of this pent up energy. She wouldn't even miss him.

The thought only made him more frustrated.

Noelle lay on her bed thinking over the day. Linc was right, she probably wouldn't mourn Trevor forever. Life moved on. But she wanted more time to grieve his loss. He'd been so very special to her. Trevor had been a wonderful husband–as long as it went with the way he wanted things. A truly indulgent husband would have found a house together, allowed her more say in their furnishings. And given her free rein to try her women's safety idea in the company like Linc had.

She rolled over and pushed the disloyal thoughts away. Yet another sprang into place. One she'd thought about before.

What would her life be like if Linc had asked her out first?

9

Noelle couldn't concentrate. Giving up after several minutes, she went out to the living room. Linc wasn't around. Spying the newspaper he'd brought in that morning, she scooped it up and turned to the classified section. The sooner she found another place to live, the sooner she'd get her equilibrium back.

She was overwhelmed by the number of listings. She recognized a couple of locations, but most were completely foreign to her. She needed someone to help decipher the listings and let her know which locations would be best suited for her.

Linc came to mind, but she thought he'd balk at the suggestion. He seemed content to have her stay in his guest room indefinitely.

Taking care of her for Trevor, she knew.

She'd take the classifieds in with her in the morning and see what advice Betty could give.

Tossing the paper aside, she leaned back on the sofa. Had Linc gone to take a nap? It didn't sound like him.

Feeling restless, Noelle rose and went to unpack the backpack. There was little food left, but all the trash needed to be disposed of and she could put the blanket in with things to wash before returning it to the linen closet.

That chore took less than five minutes.

Where was Linc?

Had he gone out again? She went to his bedroom door. It was closed most of the way, but not latched. She knocked. When there was no response, she pushed it open. The room was empty. He had gone out.

"He's perfectly entitled to do anything he wants," she murmured, feeling neglected. "He doesn't need to babysit me."

But after the entire day in his company, she missed him. Just as a friend, of course.

Darn it, she wished he'd never told her he'd wanted to ask her out way back when. It was all she could think about. That and the promise he'd made Trevor. Was his helpfulness now due to that promise or was he truly interested in her?

How could he be and date other women? She better not fool herself into thinking there was anything to Linc's attention. Maybe he'd had some fleeting interest in her six years ago, but that was a long time. He wasn't a monk. She remembered Trevor commenting time and again on the variety of women Linc dated.

She wondered what the woman had been like he'd taken to dinner last night. What kind of relationship did the two of them have?

Irritated that she was even thinking about that, she went back to her room and picked up her phone. Time for a reality check. She'd call her friend Marian and see what was happening back in Washington. Marian was always up to the minute on all the gossip. Noelle needed some of that right now.

"So how's San Francisco?" Marian asked when she heard Noelle's voice.

"Okay. My apartment building got burned and I'm back to sharing Linc's space."

"Are you okay?"

"Yes, it wasn't my apartment, but another one on a different floor. But there was tons of water damage and they say it'll be months before the place is habitable again. So until then I'm virtually homeless."

"Kismet."

"What?"

"Fate. I think you two are destined to be together."

"Don't be silly. Linc was Trevor's business partner. He's just being helpful. Rents are through the roof out here. He has a spare room no one was using, so he offered it to me."

"Yeah, right. He could have put you up in a hotel, so don't give me that."

"Marian, I called to be cheered up, not to have someone play long-distance matchmaker."

"Why not? You're single again."

"I am still mourning my husband," Noelle said stiffly.

Did everyone forget Trevor so easily?

"I know, sweetie. It's so sad. Trevor was a great guy. But you knew before his death he was going. He made you promise to move on in life. Live up to it."

"So soon?"

"Is there a law against soon?"

"I'm not ready."

She might never be ready for someone like Linc.

"I'm not saying marry the guy. But if he wants to show you a good time, go for it. Get some happiness back into your life. Those last weeks with Trevor were so draining. And I know from what you said before, Paul has been a pain. You're in a new place, so make new friends and live a little."

"Linc kissed me," she blurted out.

"Whoa. He did? How was it?"

"Fantastic," Noelle said reluctantly.

Why had she blurted that out? It was like throwing gasoline on a fire. Marian would never give up on matchmaking with this information.

"See, I told you. The only time I saw his picture—the one with him and Trevor getting that award?—I thought he was gorgeous. Is he in real life?"

"Oh, yes. He's gorgeous and sexy and dynamic and intense. Sometimes when he looks at me I feel I'm the only person in the world."

"Maybe the only person in *his* world," Marian suggested.

"I don't think so. I think he's honoring a promise to Trevor. I just hope Trevor didn't bring up marriage."

"What?"

"I didn't tell you, but before he died, Trevor suggested one time that Linc and I marry. I mean, friendship is one thing and asking his partner to watch out for me is even acceptable, but marriage?"

"Do you think Linc would do such a thing? Marry just because his partner wanted him to?"

"Normally I wouldn't think so. Linc is very much his own man. But he and Trevor had a special bond and I sometimes think Linc feels Trevor was responsible for the company taking off like it has. I don't. From what I saw once I joined the firm, Linc was the driving force. But if he felt obligated who knows."

"Interesting he's never married," Marian pointed out.

"He dates. He went on a date last night."

"With you staying there?"

"He made the date before the apartment building burned and I moved back. I have no ties on him—he's free to date anyone he wants."

"But?"

"But nothing."

"Come on, Noelle, this is your old friend Marian. Don't tell me but nothing."

"I shouldn't be jealous."

"Oh, girl, you aren't falling for him, are you?"

"No. I don't think so."

"Hey, it's okay if you do. He's available, sexy, successful. What's not to like about him?"

Noelle finally verbalized the thought that had most gripped her. "How would I ever know if he was interested in me for me or because of a promise to Trevor?"

Noelle was still puzzling over that question twenty minutes later when she heard Linc return.

Her conversation with Marian hadn't been particularly settling. She almost wished she hadn't called her friend except she had enjoyed sharing the problem. Not that Marian's suggestion was helpful—she said go for it.

"Noelle?" Linc called from the hall.

She went to open her bedroom door.

"I'm here," she said, stepping into the hall.

Linc had obviously gone for that run he'd started that morning. He was damp with perspiration. His T-shirt was molded to his chest, displaying the firm muscles that didn't come from working behind a desk.

"I called for dinner. Food should arrive by the time I'm done with my shower, but be on the lookout for it in case it comes earlier than expected, okay? There's money on the chest by the door."

She nodded, fascinated about every aspect of this man.

He went into his bedroom and closed the door. She remained standing where she was, picturing him crossing to his bathroom, shedding the running clothes. Abruptly she turned back to her room–away from the thoughts flooding her mind.

Linc came out as the doorbell rang. He continued to the front door and entered the living room a couple of minutes later with an assortment of white bags. The aroma of Chinese food made Noelle's mouth water.

"I set the table while waiting," she said. "Even brewed some hot tea to go with the meal."

"Sounds good, thanks."

They sat down and began to help themselves from the different cartons. Some dishes she recognized, a couple were unknown.

Noelle hoped Linc would eat and then go some place, though where she wasn't sure. It was his apartment, after all.

Maybe she should go to a movie or something. But she still didn't know her way around the city well enough to find a movie theater at this time of night.

"You read the paper?" he asked, glancing at the sections of the Sunday paper scattered near the sofa.

"Mainly the classified section. I was looking for an apartment. I suspect I'll never get back into the building."

He didn't say anything.

Perversely she was annoyed he kept silent. She'd prepared for an argument.

"I need to get a place of my own," she clarified.

"Good idea. We'll get Betty on it tomorrow," he said, taking some more of the kung pao chicken.

"Fine."

She took another bite, confused. Maybe she'd misread the entire setup. Couldn't she get anything straight when it concerned Linc?

By Friday of the following week, Noelle still hadn't found an apartment. She was too busy at work to devote a lot of time to visiting places to check them out, but had gone to see at least a dozen.

None suited her.

She wasn't that finicky, she knew. But either the location was poor or there were no amenities she wanted or the cost was far more than she wanted to pay.

Meantime work was booming. The requests for their women's safety services was growing. She went to speak to Linc about expanding by adding another employee for the project. He had a stack of files on his desk, his shirtsleeves rolled up.

Odd, she thought as she sat opposite him. They shared an apartment, yet she'd rarely seen him over the last two weeks. Was he avoiding her?

Next week he was off to Australia and would be gone for ten days. She'd have the apartment to herself. But she almost felt that way now.

"I haven't seen much of you," she said.

"I've been busy." He tossed his pencil on the desk and leaned back in his chair. "Is that why you're here? Because you haven't seen me?"

"No." She put her spread sheet on the desk. "I want another person on my project. We're running ragged meeting the demands. This is really taking off."

She was excited about the way things were going and felt a sense of vindication. She wished Trevor had had faith in her idea the way Linc had.

He picked up the sheet and scanned the numbers.

"Sounds fine to me. You don't need my permission to hire or fire, Noelle. You're a partner."

"Really?"

"Did you think it was a made-up thing? You got Trevor's shares. You have more than pulled your weight since you've been here–and added to the bottom line. Why the incredulity?"

"It still feels strange, I guess."

She remained seated.

"Anything else?"

Was he trying to get rid of her? What happened to the man who had kissed her so passionately the weekend before last?

"I still haven't found an apartment," she said.

"You can stay where you are as long as you like. It was your idea to move. What's the word on your current apartment?"

"I'm moving the rest of the furniture into storage. They estimated another six months or longer for repairs. Apparently they have to come up to code on several things that slipped under the radar before."

He looked at her and shrugged. "So stay."

"We'll see. You ready for your trip to Australia?"

"Yes. Ever been?"

She shook her head.

"Nice people. When I get back, I'm scheduled to return to Vancouver. Want to go? I think there're some groups up there who would be interested in the women's safety program. You could explain ours and see if it works there as well as it's doing here in San Francisco."

"I'd love to go. When exactly? I'll have to get some new brochures made up, to reflect a different venue."

There were a dozen things that popped into mind to work on if they were expanding the project to another city.

Wouldn't her team be excited!

He mentioned a date toward the end of the month.

She nodded. "Thanks, Linc. It'll be terrific." She rose.

"Noelle. I'm not taking anyone out this weekend, if you wanted to cook dinner again on Saturday night," he said.

It was amazing how that casual comment had the ability to raise her spirits even more.

"I'd love to. How about lasagna and all the trimmings?"

"My mouth is watering already," he said with a lopsided smile.

She left, trying to ignore the catch in her heart with that killer smile.

They seemed to be back on their normal terms. She hoped it stayed that way.

Just before she was ready to call it a day, her phone rang. It was Paul Simpson.

"What do you want now, Paul?" she asked, exasperated with his constantly harassing her.

"I sent your lawyer highlighted sections of the trust. You'll see some of the jewelry was in the trust and shouldn't have been given away."

"I'll let my attorney decide that. Trevor gave them to me, he must have thought they were his to do with as he wished."

"Trevor wasn't thinking straight. He hadn't been for a long time, if you asked me."

No one did, she thought.

"He was right about you, though," Paul said snidely.

"What are you talking about?"

"That guy who worked with him, Linc Mathias. As soon as Trevor died, you up and leave for California."

"If I had a home to remain in, I might have stayed in Virginia. But you'll remember that was also part of the trust and you couldn't wait for me to clear out."

"Convenient, I'd say. As an excuse to move to California. How is Linc these days? It's too bad Trevor couldn't have known you'd head there the minute he was gone," Paul said unpleasantly.

"Because of business—and Trevor wanted me to come."

"So you say," he replied.

"Why else?"

"To be with Linc, of course. Trevor knew sooner or later you'd turn to a younger man."

"That's not so!"

"Trevor wasn't dead two months before you joined the younger partner in that firm."

Noelle took a deep breath. She didn't like what Paul was insinuating.

"Linc and I have a working relationship. Nothing more."

She dismissed the kisses instantly. She'd never tell Paul about those. Who knew how he'd interpret that?

"You could have stayed in D.C. Trevor was right to send Mathias as far away as he could once he started dating you."

"What are you talking about now?"

"From the moment you started seeing Trevor, he worried you'd turn to a younger man. Surely you knew that? Though I will say you played your cards well. He was as besotted with you the day he died as he was when he first married you. Did you expect then to have him die so soon? He was decades older than you. Too bad there wasn't more you could have taken from the estate."

"Stop it, Paul. I'm not listening to this. Do not call again."

"Too busy with Linc, huh? Trevor was right to get him away. Look how fast you went after him after Trevor died," he said again.

"*Goodbye*, Paul." Noelle hung up the phone.

How dare he keep calling her and making insinuations.

She'd been a loving and loyal wife to Trevor.

She frowned. Granted, she'd always felt an awkwardness around Linc after she and Trevor began dating. And now she was so aware of the man she could hardly keep two thoughts in her mind. But there had never been anything between them while she was married to Trevor.

Still, she now suspected that she was one of the reasons Linc had left to open an office in California–because she was dating Trevor instead of him.

But had Trevor really been jealous of Linc? Had he suspected her of being interested in his partner?

Noelle was horrified.

No, Paul had made it all up to upset her.

She rose and went to Linc's office. The door was open so she peeked inside. He sat at his desk, the stack of papers even larger than earlier.

"Got a minute?" she asked.

"Sure. What's up?"

"I just had another call from Paul. He said Trevor sent you to California to get you away from me."

Linc didn't say anything, just looked at her.

"Is it true?"

He looked at the folders on his desk. "We decided it could be beneficial to open a West Coast office," he said slowly.

"At the exact moment when Trevor and I became engaged?" she pushed.

"The timing seemed right."

"Did Trevor suggest it?"

He met her eyes, then nodded once.

"Because?"

"We wanted to expand the business."

Noelle stepped closer to the desk. "Is that the *only* reason?"

"The only one that mattered."

"So Paul was right. Trevor didn't trust me."

She sat on the visitor's chair, looking back on her marriage that she'd thought was so perfect.

"Trevor trusted you."

"Don't lie."

Anger flashed briefly in Linc's eyes. "I never lie," he said with steely determination.

"So why did you set up the West Coast office at that particular time?"

"Leave it, Noelle. What does it matter? We established the office here and it did even better than the Washington one."

"Why then?" she insisted.

For a moment she thought he wouldn't answer but then he said,

"It wasn't that Trevor didn't trust you. He just wanted you to himself, without competition, so he said."

"What, he was afraid you and I would start an affair or something? He didn't know me at all if he thought that."

"Or me, unless you think I would do something like that?" he asked.

"Of course not. I never even knew you were thinking of asking me out. You never gave a clue."

"Or you didn't pick up on them and Trevor did."

"What?"

"Look, it's history. He wanted a clear field. He was my friend, so I left."

"I can't believe he didn't trust me," she repeated.

"It wasn't that."

"Of course it was. And now Paul thinks the minute Trevor died, I took off to be with you. Oh Lord, don't let him find out I'm staying at your apartment!"

"Staying is the key word. A temporary arrangement until your apartment is habitable again or you find a new one. Trevor knew you loved him, Noelle."

"But did he know me? I never thought he shouldn't see his friends because he might fall for one of the women. How could he have thought that of me?"

"Cut him some slack, Noelle," Linc said. "You were almost thirty years younger than he was. Of course he was going to feel insecure when younger men came around. In the normal way of things, like draws to like."

"You thought I married him for his money. Did everyone think that?"

"Trevor didn't and he's the only one who counted."

She wasn't sure how she felt–deflated, depressed. She knew why Paul disliked her so much; he'd never thought she'd loved his brother. And deliberately or not, Trevor had fed that concept by removing all competition as if Noelle couldn't be trusted to be faithful if any younger men were around.

Suddenly she looked at Linc, anger growing.

"That's why most of the operatives in Washington were Trevor's age. Or female. He really didn't trust me."

"Most were older because they had the experience we

wanted. Don't let Paul's comments color the past. You and Trevor were happy, remember that."

"That's why you only came to visit twice in six years. Trevor always came here—and usually alone."

Linc shrugged.

"He knew I was floored when you started dating him. He must have picked up on my interest and thought that out of sight would be out of mind."

"Did it work?"

"What do you think?"

Noelle was shaken by his answer. She wished she knew for sure. Wished she knew how she felt especially in light of this latest twist.

She couldn't get beyond the fact that Trevor had not trusted in her love.

"I think I'm going home now," she said, rising.

"Wait five minutes and I'll drive you."

"Actually, I'm going to walk. I need some time to myself to deal with this."

"It's not as big a deal as you're making it. He loved you very much. He just had trouble believing you loved him back in the same way because of the age difference."

"And he wanted to make sure nothing tested that love, so he'd never know for sure. Did he worry every day we were married? Did my telling him I loved him mean nothing to him? It *is* a big deal, Linc. To me, at least."

Noelle left, only stopping by her office to get her coat and purse. The foundations of her marriage had been shaken. And she wasn't sure how to deal with the hurt. Trevor was no longer around to confront. She had to accept the fact he'd never fully trusted in her love.

What a bitter thing to swallow when he was gone and couldn't be reassured. Her heart ached for his uncertainty. She wished she'd known. Could she have done something further to convince him?

Linc watched her walk away. Dammit, Trevor, he thought. You should have had more faith in Noelle. And in me.

He rose and walked to the window, staring sightlessly at the view. Trevor had definitely sensed Linc's interest.

He'd out and out told him one time he was worried Noelle would grow tired of an older man and look at a man more her age. He couldn't help the other men who might come into her life, but he could deal with Linc. Either he could leave Washington or Trevor was quitting the firm.

"I never would have risked our friendship in that way," Linc murmured.

He'd been attracted to their new secretary from the first day. But he hadn't known her long, nor had the bond with her been as strong as the one he had with Trevor. Trevor had been an integral part of the firm. It would not be the success it was today without him.

So Linc had walked away without saying a word to Noelle and left Trevor to the young girl who loved him.

Linc thought back to those first weeks in San Francisco. Twice he'd almost said to forget it and headed back to Virginia to see if he could interest Noelle in a younger man. But he owed Trevor too much. And as time went on, he'd thought he'd got over his infatuation with her and strengthened his friendship with Trevor.

Trevor had mentioned Noelle from time to time, to point out how happy they were, and that Linc had been wrong to attribute mercenary motives to her. Even Linc had seen that when year after year Noelle had appeared happy in her marriage.

Now that happiness was tarnished.

Trevor should have trusted her. And if it hadn't worked out, he would have known he'd given it his best shot.

Had Trevor feared Noelle's leaving every day? From what Linc knew of Noelle, she was too loyal for that.

He hoped he didn't come out on the wrong end of the stick in this situation. Could he say or do anything to make her feel better? The disillusioned look on her face when she left tore at his heart.

Blast Paul to kingdom come. Why did he persist in bothering her? Maybe Linc should have a talk with the man himself and make a few things clear.

The first being that Paul needed to leave Noelle alone. Most of the damage had been done already, however. If Linc could keep him from calling her again, or sending detectives, it'd be worth the confrontation.

He'd made a special effort over the last couple of weeks to stay away from her. The kisses had been almost more than he could stand and they were not enough. He wanted more. He wanted Noelle in every way a man wanted a woman.

He didn't lie, as he'd told her, so that was the reason for a counter question, rather than answering hers. Let her think what she would. He wasn't ready to tell her how much he wanted her. She was too skittish.

He was worried their kisses would cause her to run in the other direction, so he was trying to cool things down a bit. Take it slowly.

But Vancouver would give them a chance to be away from the office, away from daily routines, and spend time together. It was also over Thanksgiving. The first since Trevor died.

He didn't want her to give into sad memories. Being in a foreign country, the holiday wouldn't be observed. He hoped the trip would help her get through the day without sadness.

For Christmas, he wondered if she'd consider going with him to Cancun.

"Dreamer," he said, pushing away from the window.

He was heading for home. He wanted to be there when she arrived.

10

Noelle walked briskly along the sidewalk trying to erase the emotions that churned inside her. She couldn't believe Trevor had doubted her. He was as bad as his brother. Had Paul's poisoned ideas taken root and grown in Trevor's mind?

She was furious with the facts she'd just learned. Angry and sad. How awful if her husband lived in fear of her leaving every day of their marriage. She couldn't imagine how that would affect a person.

She was almost as angry with Linc. How dare he meekly leave as if the idea Trevor feared had any basis in truth? Both she and Linc were honorable people and would never have done anything underhanded. It was another slap from Trevor to both of them.

She was frankly amazed that Linc had given in. She would have expected him to stand up and tell Trevor to take his idea and shove it. And then storm from the office.

Maybe he had.

San Francisco is a city of hills. By the time Noelle had climbed California Street, she was out of breath. She was within blocks of the apartment and didn't feel any calmer. Instead of heading home, she went to the park near Grace

Cathedral and sat on one of the benches. The afternoon sun lingered but the air was cool. She shivered slightly, knowing the sun would be setting before long and the temperatures would really drop.

The most frustrating aspect of the entire situation was that she couldn't do anything about it. Trevor had lived and died believing what he believed.

She could be angry at Linc but when she thought about it, he'd done a gallant thing by leaving the field wide open for his partner and friend. She'd stay mad at Paul, on general principles if nothing else. He hadn't liked her before and she knew nothing would ever change that. It was not something she'd let bother her any more.

Gradually her anger faded. Only the sorrow for Trevor remained.

How had she been so blind she had missed that distrust? She thought back over their years together. Most of their friends had been Trevor's, older married couples who had been his friends for years. She'd kept two or three close girlfriends, but she and Trevor together rarely did anything with them. At the time Noelle had thought it normal for a new wife to blend in with her husband's life.

His house, his friends, his life. Had Noelle simply become lost in Trevor?

A gust of wind made her shiver. Rising, she turned toward Linc's apartment and started walking. This time the brisk pace was to get warm.

Noelle let herself into the apartment a few minutes later, pausing near the door and listening for Linc.

"I'm in the kitchen," he called out.

She hung up her coat and headed there.

He was looking in a phone directory. Glancing up, he pointed to an item on the page. "I thought we could order Italian food from Giovanni's. What would you like?"

"I can cook dinner," she said.

In fact she'd relish the chance to get her mind off the recent revelation.

"I thought you could use a break, some pampering."

She looked at him.

"Are you all right? Guys never think women need pampering."

He shrugged. "You had bad news, so why not let me make dinner for us?"

"I'd rather go out," she said perversely.

"Sounds good to me—saves cleaning up anyway. I'm ready if you are."

Now that he offered, she felt like saying no and staying home.

Although going out might be best. Maybe she needed to get out into a crowd so she could forget for a little while.

"I'll wash my hands and be ready myself."

The small Italian restaurant in North Beach was almost empty. So much for being in a crowd. They got a table near the front and soon ordered. Linc looked at her when the waiter left.

"Did your walk home do you any good?" he asked.

"It helped me see that no matter what the truth of the situation was I can't change Trevor's perception. I'm still mad at Trevor and you, but I'll get over it."

"Mad at *me?* Why? I didn't do anything."

"You left because he asked you to. Why didn't you stand up for yourself? You know you'd never have made a play for me if I was married to Trevor. He insulted you as well as me."

"It was time to expand," Linc said. "Like up to Vancouver."

She shook her head. "Changing the subject?"

"Yes. It seems to me we're done with the other topic. You'll like Vancouver, it reminds me a lot of San Francisco—clean, near the water, friendly people. And there's a large Asian community. The men we'll be meeting with on Thursday are originally from Hong Kong, and relocated to Vancouver before the Chinese took over from the British."

"Is my position in the firm a made-up one?" Noelle asked suddenly, wondering if the new project was as a result of Trevor's edict to "take care of Noelle."

Linc's eyes narrowed slightly in anger.

"I'm not the bad guy here. And I certainly wouldn't make up some job merely to keep you occupied. There's enough work and money coming in that I could pay you to stay away from the firm. You had a good idea with the women's safety issue and it's proving to be a good direction for us to take. How can you ask if it's a made-up job?"

"I think I'm feeling insecure about everything after learning what I did today."

"Noelle."

She looked at him.

"You're a competent, insightful professional. You're

making a contribution to the company. When I can, I'll buy you out. Or you can stay. The choice is yours."

For an instant, Noelle wondered what Trevor would have thought. He'd have had an opinion for sure.

Yet as Linc said, the choice was hers. Every choice hereafter was hers.

"Okay, then. Tell me more about Vancouver."

Linc told her about the hotel he liked, right on the bay. How he spent hours in Stanley Park, running, or enjoying the beauty so close to the downtown area of the city.

When he moved the topic of conversation onto the business side of things, he was amused to see her light up. She'd been interested in Vancouver, but seemed to thrive on discussing the challenges of the company.

Trevor made mistakes with Noelle. One had been holding her back to an administrative role when she had good ideas to grow the company. Another had been to doubt her loyalty and fidelity.

Linc wasn't going to make the same mistakes. He wanted her, no mistake, but if he couldn't have her, he still wanted her to live up to all her potential, to grow, flourish and find happiness.

Darn, he was starting to sound like he was bidding her goodbye.

"We'll fly up to Vancouver on Tuesday, meet with them on Wednesday and Thursday, then I thought we'd stay a few more days so you can see that part of British Columbia. It's beautiful country."

"That's Thanksgiving week, did you know?"

He nodded. "I'm not much on holidays."

"Where's your family?"

"My grandparents died before I moved here. Holidays don't mean as much without family."

She studied him for a moment. "So you joined the military when young. I bet it became your family for a while. Then you used to spend holidays with Trevor, didn't you? That changed after we married."

"I was in San Francisco by then," he shrugged, not wanting to get into that again.

The waiter arrived with their steaming plates, arranging them with a flourish at their places. He poured some red wine, checked to make sure everything was satisfactory and left.

"I know you're probably used to a traditional Thanksgiving feast, but will you mind being in Canada instead?" he asked.

She shook her head.

"No but I think you deliberately arranged this. The first holiday without a loved one is hard. I remember from when my aunt died. You knew I lived with her growing up, didn't you?"

He nodded. He'd heard a lot from Trevor over the years.

"Your parents never married and your mother left you with her sister when you were about six, right?"

She nodded. "Aunt Helen was wonderful. I never thought of her as anything but my mother."

"Have you ever heard from your actual mother?"

She shook her head. "I didn't even know where to contact her when I was getting married. I'm sorry I didn't have children, though. I would never have treated them like my mother did me."

"You sound as if you're a hundred years old. You're young enough to have a dozen children if you want."

"Unlike my mother, I believe in being married to have children," she snapped.

"So marry again," he countered.

"What are the odds of finding another man to love after having Trevor?"

"I'd say the odds are terrific," he replied. "You're young, pretty, interesting to be with."

Sexy and desirable, but those thoughts he kept to himself. He glanced around, wondering if the other men in the restaurant were as intrigued by her loveliness as he was. He could understand Trevor's wanting to keep her sheltered—away from temptation—not because he doubted her loyalty, but to keep a cherished object safe.

Only Noelle wasn't a cherished object, but a vital woman who made Linc start dreaming about things that would likely never be, especially in light of their history.

She didn't respond.

"I think you should plan on marrying again," he said.

She frowned.

"I don't know. What if I don't fall in love again? Or if I do, how would I know if my husband loves me? I thought Trevor did and look at what I found out today."

"He *did* love you."

"We never had children. Do you think he suspected he wouldn't live long enough to see them grow up?"

Linc shrugged. What he suspected was that Trevor hadn't wanted to give up his lifestyle. He liked having a young wife to do things with and didn't want that to change with a new baby in the family.

He changed the subject again. He wasn't comfortable talking about her and Trevor's marriage. Or any marriage for that matter. He didn't have a lot of experience in happy unions.

"How's Betty working out as a trainer instead of secretary?" he asked, hoping to defuse the tension that seemed to be building between them. The last thing he wanted was Noelle to be dwelling on Trevor and the past. He wanted her to focus on the future.

"She's a natural. Knows all about the business, took to training like she'd been born for it, and is one of our best representatives. She also lives alone and has incorporated some of our suggestions already which makes it easy to talk about with assurance."

Linc began to eat his veal scallopini while he listened to Noelle.

Betty wasn't the only natural. She almost glowed with excitement about the new division in the company. He'd made a good choice and liked knowing she was doing something she enjoyed so much.

When dinner was finished they headed back to the apartment. Almost like a married couple, Linc thought wryly.

What would it be like to be married to Noelle? To see her every morning, hold her every night, make love to her whenever the mood struck?

Pushing that tempting thought away he concentrated on driving.

"Thanks for dinner, Linc," she said as they rode the elevator to his floor. "It was just what I needed to get some perspective. Whatever the status of my marriage was, it's over now. If I ever think to take that step again, I'll look long and hard at the relationship to make sure I know how my future husband feels."

Noelle bid Linc goodnight and went to her room. She wanted an early night so she'd be fresh in the morning. She had a couple of weeks to get everything together for the presentation in Vancouver. She wished Linc wasn't going to be gone during that time.

She'd miss him while he was gone. She was used to getting rides to the office and home. Sharing dinners and standing clear from him in the mornings as he went straight for the coffee. He wasn't someone to mess with before he had his coffee.

Better get used to being alone in the apartment, she warned herself. Her own would be repaired before many more months or she'd find a new one and return to single living.

At least she'd see Linc every day—when he was in the office.

If he weren't leaving for Australia this week, would he be inviting another woman out on a date? She had no hold on him. If he wanted to date a dozen women, that was his privilege.

Only, Noelle wished he wanted to date her.

She sat up in bed. Where had that thought come from?

From the attraction she always felt around him, from the intensity with which he seemed to listen to her, understand her. From his encouragement and support, which had enabled her to grow in ways she'd only dreamed about before.

She knew she was crazy about Linc Mathias. Was it more than admiration and sexual awareness? What would it be like to spend the rest of her life with him? Partners in business *and* at home?

She shivered and got up, pacing the small space of her bedroom. She was acting like a teenager with a huge crush on the football quarterback. Linc was her friend—her late husband's friend. How could any relationship possibly work between them?

It was a good thing he was leaving soon, she needed the time to get her head on straight. Trevor had suggested she think about marriage to Linc—as a means to keep the business together and because he didn't like thinking about her alone.

But she was proving she could manage her life just fine. She liked San Francisco. Loved her job. And Linc had said it wasn't a made-up position.

Noelle smiled as she thought again about the women's safety project. It was making money, providing a service, and expanding. Linc was right, it was an important feature of their business now.

His only kindness was offering her a place to stay. He'd never said a word out of place. Never given a hint—except for those kisses.

Yes, they were most definitely *not* friendly. Erotic, exciting, passionate yes, but not friendly.

She grew warm thinking about being held in his arms, his mouth moving across her cheeks or sweeping across her lips with an urgency that found a match within her. The last man she needed to get involved with was Linc. Yet he was the only man she had any interest in.

November

Noelle gazed out of the airplane window. There was a cloud layer which made the view boring. She shifted in her seat and glanced at the magazine she'd picked up at the airport. Linc was meeting her in Vancouver. His stay in Australia had been extended twice until it made sense for him to fly directly to Canada and not return to San Francisco first.

Unfortunately Noelle wasn't that great a traveler. She wished Linc had been with her to take her mind off flying. Glancing out the window again she noticed the wing was still attached. Not being able to see the ground was probably a good thing, she thought. Maybe she'd suggest they take the train home.

Vancouver's airport was crowded. She waited for her luggage, waited to get a cab and then waited in traffic as they inched toward downtown. Linc had arrived a few hours ago. He must be exhausted coming in from Australia. Would he want to have dinner together?

Arriving later than she'd expected at the hotel, Noelle had no difficulty checking in. When she reached her room, she called Linc.

The phone rang several times before being answered by a muffled voice.

"Linc? It's Noelle, I just got here."

Suddenly it registered.

"You were sleeping, weren't you. I'm sorry, I know you must be tired. I didn't mean to wake you."

"No problem. Glad you made it. We're scheduled to meet with the client at nine in the morning. Want to meet for breakfast at seven? We can go over the presentation."

"Sure, that'd be fine."

Disappointment whipped through her. She'd seriously missed Linc these last four weeks. She'd been anticipating seeing him again and now he wanted to wait until morning. Well, she guessed that put her in her place.

"G'night," he said and hung up.

One thing she'd learned over the last few months was patience. He obviously wasn't as anxious to see her. She'd be professional, courteous and friendly. And if he came close enough to kiss her she'd deck him.

Linc waited impatiently by the elevator the next morning. He'd called her room right before he left his to tell her he was leaving. He thought they'd arrive in the hotel lobby at the same time. Four other elevator cars doors had slid open and then closed again after the people stepped off. None was Noelle.

He'd blown it last night. He could have gotten up, taken her to dinner, talked to her about how his trip to Australia had gone. But he'd been exhausted from being up more than twenty-four hours and knew he'd be lousy company. Still, it might have been worth it to see her earlier. He hadn't gotten her room number or he could go up and knock on her door—

The elevator at the far end opened its doors and Noelle stepped out. She was dressed in a cherry-red suit, white lace at the deep vee of the jacket. Her hair shone beneath the artificial light. She looked good enough to scoop up and take far away where no one could ever find them. For a minute Linc considered doing just that.

"Good morning," she said.

There didn't appear to be any welcome in her cool gaze. Was she still upset?

"Have a good trip up?" he asked.

He wanted to take her in his arms and kiss her, ask if she'd missed him as much as he'd missed her. But there was a barrier between them that hadn't been there before. What had changed over the last few weeks?

"Uneventful. How was the flight in from Sydney?"

"Long. We had engine trouble out of Honolulu, so we turned back and ended up coming on a different plane."

He noticed her start when he'd mentioned the engine trouble.

"Are you all right?" she asked politely.

"I'm fine. How are you?"

"Fine."

"I don't think so," he said, drawing her to one side out of the path of others coming from the elevators.

"What do you mean?"

The first bit of animation lit her face when she looked up at him.

"Let's start over. Good morning, Noelle, I missed you," Linc said, dropping his briefcase and pulling her into his arms to kiss her.

Her resistance lasted about six seconds then she melted against him, returning his kiss with fervor. She was so feminine and sweet-smelling. Her mouth enticed him as he deepened the kiss. He'd missed her every day he'd been gone. It was time to find out how much she missed him.

When he realized the kiss was getting dangerously out of hand, he pulled back, gazing with satisfaction at her bemused expression.

Reaching down to scoop up both briefcases, he kept a grip on her arm and led her to an elevator just about to close. Slipping inside, he was pleased to see it was empty. Dropping the cases, he punched the button for the top floor and again pulled her into his embrace.

When the elevator stopped, the doors opened.

Noelle pulled back and looked at the empty hall. "Is this your floor?" she asked.

"No, but it'll do."

He lifted the briefcases once more and stepped out. She followed.

"Well, when you travel, you sure are glad to see a friend in a foreign setting," she said as the door closed behind them, leaving them in the deserted hall.

"I'm testing a theory," he said, studying her.

Her mouth was slightly swollen and rosy. Her eyes

sparkled. Her hair was mussed. And he wanted her badly.

She must have read something in his gaze, because she snapped up a hand, palm out and backed away a step.

"Hold on, Linc. What's going on?"

"I'm trying a theory," he repeated slowly.

"A theory."

"That you missed me as much as I missed you."

She licked her lips. "Of course I missed you. The office is always quiet when you're gone."

"I'm not talking about the office."

"Oh." She visibly swallowed. "What are you talking about?"

"You and me."

Noelle took a deep breath. "You and me? As in partners in the firm?"

"Among other things."

"What other things?"

He stepped closer, reaching out to take a tress of hair in his fingers, enjoying the softness. His eyes looked deep in hers. Was he seeing what was really there? Or what he wanted so desperately to see?

"I was going to wait, but I'm tired of waiting."

"For what?" she asked.

"To ask you to marry me," Linc said.

Noelle stared at him, horror growing.

Linc wished he could take back the words. Her reaction was nothing like he'd expected, hoped for.

"I *knew* it!" she said, stepping back. "Paul called you, didn't he? This is some convoluted way to try to help me. I won't have it. No, I *won't*."

She walked part way down the hall, spun and came back.

"I can handle Paul Simpson myself. I can live my life just fine without some man taking care of me. I will *not* marry you."

"I've hardly spoken with Paul since the funeral. What's he doing now?" Linc asked.

Maybe there was some misunderstanding they could easily clear up.

"Threatening to challenge Trevor's will. Let him. It was first written five years ago, long before he became ill. There was no undue persuasion, no counter indicative medical problems that would have affected his judgment. Paul doesn't have a leg to stand on."

"I *haven't* talked to Paul," Linc insisted.

"Then why are you asking me to marry you?" She frowned. "Trevor put you up to it—didn't he?

"Trevor's dead," Linc said gently.

"You know he told me he thought we should consider getting married. If you think I need you to go to such lengths just to honor some dying man's request, then you can think again. We need to get to breakfast and then to the meeting."

She pressed the elevator call button and resolutely faced the doors.

"I'm not honoring some request of Trevor's. He never suggested to me that I marry you. It's probably the last thing he really wanted."

"Then why did you say that?" she asked, looking at him over her shoulder.

"Because I want you to marry me," he said simply.

Noelle felt as if the world tilted.

The elevator arrived just as a door down the hall opened. A man emerged, saw the elevator and called, "Hold that for me, would you?"

She stepped in and held the door. Linc followed. A moment later the other man joined them. Noelle pressed the lobby button and silently the three of them descended, stopping on two other floors to pick up other guests of the hotel.

When they reached the ground floor, Noelle stepped out and turned in the direction of the main lobby. Linc caught up in a moment.

"I guess the answer is no then," he said, slipping her briefcase handle into her hand.

"You can't be serious," she said, head held high as she walked toward the restaurant.

"Why would you think that?"

"We're friends. Business partners. I know Trevor asked you to watch out for me, and you feel honor bound to do that. But marriage is rather extreme. Especially when I don't need help."

He stopped and looked around. "This is a hell of a place for a proposal. No privacy, no romantic setting. I know women put store in that kind of thing."

She watched him warily. "Women also want love."

"You've got that."

She blinked. "From you?"

"Of course."

"You never said anything!"

"I just did."

She put one fist on her hip. "No, you still haven't said you love me. And how would I know if it was true or not? Remember what I found out about Trevor a little while ago."

Linc checked his watch. "We have enough time to get a quick meal and find a cab to take us to the meeting. Shall we continue this discussion later?"

"Or never," she muttered, continuing toward the restaurant.

Was the man out of his mind? He'd kissed her, granted. But he probably kissed lots of women. Like the one he'd taken on a date a few weeks ago.

Linc had done everything he could to make her life easier, from giving her an active role in the company, to putting her up while her apartment was being repaired. But not once had she seen anything from him that indicated he was madly, passionately in love with her.

And that's what she wanted in another marriage. She wanted to know her husband trusted her implicitly, loved her completely.

As she loved him.

Cringing mentally, Noelle looked away, afraid Linc would see some of her feelings reflected in her expression. She'd missed him totally while he'd been gone. Realized the awareness around him had more than just sexual overtones. He made her feel secure, confident. He gave her courage to face the future. Being with him brought her a mix of joy and happiness that she'd never felt before. All of which she'd realized when he'd been gone this last time on a trip that was too long.

To marry him—it could be wonderful.

But dare she risk it?

Not with another man who had his own agenda. She wanted love. All or nothing. Only nothing looked rather bleak from where she was standing.

The day was interminable. Her first foreign assignment and she impatiently wanted it over. The women she spoke with were very interested in learning more about their services. Noelle should have been on top of the world, but she wasn't.

Every time she glanced at Linc, he was watching her. Every time she felt her heart rate triple, she knew he was inches away.

She'd made up her mind, but her body seemed to betray every thought. She knew she had to keep her distance, but she longed for another kiss, another brush of his fingers against her cheek or his mouth on hers.

She shook her head, trying to focus on the meeting. But thoughts of Linc filled her. How long before this meeting ended?

Despite her best efforts, hope began to blossom within her. Maybe Linc did love her. Maybe he really wanted to marry her, not as a promise to Trevor, but to share the future together.

Keyed-up, she could hardly sit still in the cab ride back to the hotel.

"I thought we could rent a car and drive to Whistler on

Friday. It's a pretty town not too far away," Linc said as the driver mastered the late afternoon traffic.

"Sounds nice," she said.

What about his marriage proposal? She felt as if it stood between them, filling the cab. Would he bring it up again or was it up to her this time?

When they reached the hotel, Linc offered to meet her at seven for dinner.

"I think we have unfinished business to discuss now," Noelle said, not able to wait until after dinner to resolve things.

"If you like. Your place or mine?"

"Yours," she said firmly.

If things went bad, she could leave.

Once inside his hotel room, Noelle placed her briefcase on a chair and turned to face him.

He watched her warily.

"About your proposal," she started, hoping he'd say something.

He nodded.

"You meant it?"

"Of course. I don't say things I don't mean, you know that."

"You do love me?"

"I love you," he said. The sincerity rang in his voice.

Her heart stuttered. For a moment she believed.

"How long have you loved me?" she asked, still not trusting the timing.

Paul must have gotten through to him, and this was Linc's

way to protect her.

"For more than six years, I think," he said softly.

Her eyes met his. "*What?*"

"And I also think Trevor knew. That was one reason he insisted I leave. It was either relocate and keep the firm going or he was going to pull out."

"Trevor knew you *loved* me?"

"I wasn't sure myself back then. But over time, I've suspected. There was no future for us, when Trevor was alive. I knew that. Sometimes I'd want to come see you so badly it was all I could do not to get on a plane to fly to Washington just to look at you from a distance," Linc said.

"I can't believe it." Noelle was floored by what she was hearing.

"I never did, but it was touch and go sometimes to see if I could resist."

"And you say you think Trevor knew?" Noelle repeated in disbelief.

"We were good friends but he didn't trust me an inch around you. I would never have deliberately hurt him. You know that and I sure hope to goodness he knew it as well. But he most likely also recognized the signs in me—especially as he felt it for you himself."

"I'd never have been unfaithful to my vows," Noelle said.

"He knew that and so did I. But faithful or not, feelings change, and he was afraid you'd see him for the old man he was and turn to me."

"So you meekly left?"

"Not so meekly actually. I wanted you and I was furious

at him for beating me to the draw and asking you out first. We had never discussed dating employees before—it hadn't come up. But he was my friend and you chose him."

Noelle thought back to those first days with the new firm. There'd always been that tingling feeling around Linc. Trevor had seen it. Were they meant to be? Or was there too much between them because of Trevor?

"So the question is, how do you feel about me?" he asked.

"Confused," she replied promptly.

His gaze never left hers.

"And in love," she added softly astonished to finally give in to the feelings she tried so hard to suppress.

He swept her into his arms, kissing her like they would never part. Noelle closed her eyes and gave her all to the embrace, delighted to be in the arms of the man she loved. Could it be that happiness would be forthcoming? She loved Linc Mathias and it looked as if he loved her as much. How amazing.

An eternity later, he pulled back long enough to gaze into her eyes.

"So is this a yes?"

She smiled slowly, feeling the warmth of his love fill her. "This is a yes," she said, reaching up to kiss him again.

Epilogue

May

Linc stood on the sidewalk watching the painters carefully apply the last coat on the trim. The house looked good.

The mailman walked down the street, delivering at each house. When he reached Linc he, too, looked at the painters.

"Almost finished," he said. "Looks good."

"Once this is done, we'll have the landscape firm in to finish the yard," Linc said.

Who'd have thought last November that he and Noelle would end up with a fixer upper home? But she'd fallen in love with it when she'd first seen it and he liked to indulge his wife. They both loved the house–though it was still months away from being the way they wanted it.

The postman handed Linc the mail and continued.

He took one more look at the house and headed inside. Noelle was hard at work on the kitchen, putting away their dishes and pans now that the renovation of that room was complete.

He shuffled the envelopes, stopping when he reached the one with a familiar return address. It was the attorneys he and Trevor had used in Washington. The letter was addressed to Noelle.

When he entered the kitchen, he smiled, the familiar feeling of contentment filling him.

"You have a letter," he said, offering it to her and giving her a quick kiss.

"Thanks. I'm just about finished here. How about we celebrate by ordering in pizza?"

She looked at the return address and frowned.

"I hope there isn't something more from Paul. I thought we'd heard the last from him," she said as she tore open the envelope.

Linc didn't say a word.

They *had* heard the last from Paul; he'd made sure of that. But he wasn't planning on telling Noelle. Let her think the man finally got tired of his stupid demands and stopped harassing her. He knew she was still picky about Trevor's request that Linc take care of her.

"Oh, my God, it's from Trevor," she said.

He looked at her. "The letter?"

Noelle nodded. "Dated a couple of weeks before he died."

She looked up at him. "Today is the first anniversary of his death, you know."

Linc nodded. He'd known and not known what to do about it. Should he have mentioned it to her? Or wait for her reaction? He still wasn't sure.

"Oh, my, listen to this," she said and began to read the letter aloud.

"Dear Noelle:

"First let me tell you how much you have meant to me

over the years. You were everything I ever wanted in a wife. You made me supremely happy the entire time we were together. I only wish our time together had been longer. I would have loved to see you as an old lady with grandchildren around you. You will make a wonderful mother and grandmother. Tell your kids about me. I regret we didn't have children so I could know if they looked like their mother, had her charming personality, or her joy of life.

"I know you've been exasperated with me lately, especially with the promises I've extracted from you and from Linc. I hope I'm doing right. I also hope by the time you get this letter that you and Linc have found each other. He loves you, Noelle, I've known it all along. Being the honorable man he is, he left the field open for me to marry you. But if he'd halfway tried, I think the outcome would have been different. I couldn't have lived without you.

"If you and Linc have not found each other, take the next plane to San Francisco and look him up. Tell him Trevor wanted the two of you to be together. Youth draws to youth, after all. Have a dozen kids and name one for me.

"I have always loved you, my darling. Be happy. Live long and love Linc the rest of your life.

"Your devoted husband, Trevor."

Noelle blinked back tears. "So he most definitely did know then."

Linc took her into his arms. "And he approved, that's even more important."

She took a deep breath and smiled up through her tears.

"I love you, Linc Mathias. You'll be happy to know I'm following Trevor's advice."

"Since we've been married two months, I already knew that."

"But did you know that we'll be having the first of those dozen kids in about seven months!"

She flung her arms around the man she loved and kissed him. "Let's name the baby Trevor if he's a boy."

She would be forever grateful for the earlier love she'd shared with Trevor, for it prepared her for the deeper, lasting love she'd always have with Linc.

If you liked **Unanticipated Reunion**, you'll love **Letters to Caroline** from my Talmadge Sisters series.

If you enjoyed **Unanticipated Reunion,** please consider leaving a review.

More books by Barbara McMahon

Sweet Reunion Romance Collection
Unexpected Reunion
Unpredictable Reunion
Unanticipated Reunion

Cowboys of Wildcat Creek
Valentine's Cowboy Rescue
Shelly and the Cowboy
Kristi's Cowboy Hero
Holly's Reluctant Cowboy
Patrice's Remarkable Cowboy

The Talmadge Sisters
Letters to Caroline
Michelle's Marriage Deal
Trusting Abby

The Harts of Texas Series
Rebel Heart
Tangled Hearts
Reckless Heart

Cowboy Heroes Series
Blue Bells on the Hill
Cowboy's Bride
One Stubborn Cowboy
Crazy About a Cowboy
Never Doubt a Cowboy
Cowboy Marshal
Summer Cowboy
Second Chance Cowboy
Movie Star Cowboy

Tropical Escape Series
Island Rendezvous
Come into the Sun
Island Paradise

Rocky Point Series
Rocky Point Legacy
Rocky Point Reunion
Rocky Point Promise
Rocky Point Hero
Rocky Point Inn
Rocky Point Dawn

The Ultimate Billionaires
The Cynical Sheikh
Falling for the Sheikh
A Sheikh of Her Own
The Unforgettable Sheikh

Sweet Romance Stand-alone Collection
Because of You
Cowboy Charade
I'll Take Forever
Jared's Promise
Mail Order Bride
Not Really Married
Sweet Meant To Be
The Cowboy Comes Home
The Paper Marriage
Trusting Jake
The Banished Bride

A Sweet Clean Christmas Romance Collection
The Christmas Cop
The Cowboy's Special Christmas
A Soldier's Christmas
A Teaspoon of Mistletoe
The Christmas Locket
A Key West Christmas